JOACHIM MASANNEK

The Wild Soccer Bunch

Translated from the German by: Helga Schier

Editor: Michael Part

Original title: Felix, der Wirbelwind
Baumhaus Verlag in the Bastei Luebbe Gmbh & Co. KG
© 2010 by Bastei Luebbe GmbH & Co. KG, Cologne
"Die Wilden Fußballkerle" TM und © dreammotion GmbH

© 2011 Wild Soccer USA, Inc.

Special thanks to:
Yonatan, Yaron, and Guy Ginsberg

Library of Congress Cataloging-in-Publication data in file.

ISBN 978-0-9844257-1-6

Published by Sole Books

Second Edition December 2011
Printed in the United States of America

Layout: Lynn M. Snyder

1098765432

578DR559, December 2011

Hi *Wild Soccer Bunch* fans!

Almost a year has passed since the first book in the series, *Kevin the Star Striker,* was introduced. I hope you had a great year, played soccer, had a lot of fun, and learned some new things along the way.

I also had a great year. I played with the U.S. National Team in the 2010 FIFA World Cup in South Africa. It was an incredible experience!

I know that a lot of you dream of playing in the World Cup. I truly believe that your dream can come true if you work hard. Remember, every soccer star was a kid once!

In soccer, as in life, you must be a good sport. You must respect your opponents and learn from your mistakes. Like the *Wild Soccer Bunch,* if you lose, you need to pick yourself up and try again. You must never lose hope and never ever give up!

Your Friend and Teammate,
Landon Donovan

JOACHIM MASANNEK

The Wild Soccer Bunch

Book 2

Diego, the Tornado

Illustrations by Jan Birck

Sole
BOOKS

TABLE OF CONTENTS

The *Wild Soccer Bunch* _ _ _ _ _ _ _ _ _ _ _ 9

The Beginning of the End_ _ _ _ _ _ _ _ _ _ _ 16

Fabio _ _ _ _ _ _ _ _ _ _ _ _ _ _ _ _ _ 25

Fabio, the Wizard_ _ _ _ _ _ _ _ _ _ _ _ _ 30

Diego is Right _ _ _ _ _ _ _ _ _ _ _ _ _ _ 40

At Heaven's Gate _ _ _ _ _ _ _ _ _ _ _ _ _ 49

It's All Over _ _ _ _ _ _ _ _ _ _ _ _ _ _ 56

Scattered in the Wind _ _ _ _ _ _ _ _ _ _ _ 60

The Applesauce Duel _ _ _ _ _ _ _ _ _ _ _ 70

Meeting at Camelot _ _ _ _ _ _ _ _ _ _ _ _ 76

Never Give Up! _ _ _ _ _ _ _ _ _ _ _ _ _ 83

An Offer You Can't Refuse_ _ _ _ _ _ _ _ _ _ 90

All Eggs in One Basket _ _ _ _ _ _ _ _ _ _ _101

The Challenge _ _ _ _ _ _ _ _ _ _ _ _ _ _105

Grass Is Red_ _ _ _ _ _ _ _ _ _ _ _ _ _ _109

The Helpful Penguin _ _ _ _ _ _ _ _ _ _ _114

The Dare _ _ _ _ _ _ _ _ _ _ _ _ _ _ _123

Judgment Day _ _ _ _ _ _ _ _ _ _ _ _ _ _131

Fabio's True Colors _ _ _ _ _ _ _ _ _ _ _ 139

Dead End _ _ _ _ _ _ _ _ _ _ _ _ _ _ _142

All's Well as Long as You're Wild _ _ _ _ _ _ _144

The *Wild Soccer Bunch*

Ahem! Excuse me? My name is Diego. Diego Hernandez. Maybe you've heard of me.

Some people call me 'Asthma,' because I have asthma. Duh! But my friends call me 'the tornado.' Speaking of my friends – we're called the *Wild Soccer Bunch*. Here's the rundown on who's on the team:

Danny, the world's fastest midfielder, he rocks. He's always in a good mood, and if you ever need advice when the chips are down, Danny is *the* go-to guy. He has the wildest ideas, and his smile always saves him in a pinch. Even from being grounded. Listen – Danny is wild! But his best friend Kevin is even wilder.

Kevin, the master dribbler, star striker, and the quickest assist east of the Rockies, fears nothing and no one. He does what he wants when he wants. And all he wants is to win. Period. He'll even pass the ball instead of scoring the goal himself if it will help the team.

But he can be ruthless, too.

Just before the last game he threw Roger and Josh off the team. He said they were not good enough. Talk about a cold shot!

Tyler would never do anything like that.

Tyler is Kevin's older brother, and he never gives up either.

But he's not a cutthroat. He's our number 10, the heart of our team, and he'll do *anything* for us. He cuts nifty passes, plays defense and attack. He always is exactly where he needs to be, but you don't see him. Tyler plays as if he is wearing an invisibility cloak.

Julian is different: Julian Fort Knox, our all-in-one defender.

If he's playing, it's like three more players are on the field. At least that's what our opponents think. They complain to the referee that Julian covers them on all four sides. They *swear* we have ten players on the field. But guess what? When the referee checks, there are only seven. Ha! It's just that Julian has possession of the ball most of the time and moves so fast, he's a blur on the field.

He'll play to Tyler, who, like Clint Dempsey, cuts a pass forward to the right wing. That's where Danny races along the sidelines, looking to Kevin to see who will score. And when he's fouled, Kevin drops to the ground, moaning, writhing in pain. But, if you look closely, you can see the grin on his face.

And that's where Alex comes in. Alex the cannon Alexander has the strongest kick in the world. But Alex doesn't say much. Actually, he doesn't talk at all. Never has, not since I've known him, not even on the phone, not even to himself. But when he executes a free kick or takes a shot at the goal, he flashes his famous silent grin and hurls the ball into the net. And sometimes the goalie flies in right along with it.

"Boom!" we all shout. And we shout "1-2-3 wild!" when he scores. The one shouting the loudest is Roger.

Roger, the hero. Roger plays soccer the way a blind man takes photographs. That's what Kevin says and he's right. But that's not what matters. Even when Kevin threw him off the team, Roger stuck up for us. He showed real loyalty.

We had lost pretty much every-thing: the life-and-death match, our field, and our honor and pride. But then Roger got Larry, our coach, to come back to the team, and then he even scored the winning goal.

You see, even a player like Roger is important. We know that now. He is a loyal and irreplaceable friend, just like Josh, our superhero. Josh is Julian's younger brother. He just turned six. Sure, he's the youngest, but he was the one who saved us. Him and Sox – Kevin and Tyler's dog, the one with ears so big he looks like a bat – he showed up at the last minute and chased Mickey the bulldozer away.

Dude, that was sick! Picture a 200-pound

jellyfish jumping over a fence. Still makes us laugh just thinking about it! And ever since that day, we knew we belonged together.

Actually, I *don't* know that. I, Diego the left forward, the tornado... have asthma... and it gets worse every day. Especially since my dad moved out. Some day, it'll get so bad, they'll throw me off the team. You see, the competition never sleeps.

We have two new guys on the team: Kyle, the invincible, and Joey. Joey's so good it's as if he puts a spell on the ball. And anyone who scores a goal against Kyle will end up in the *Guinness Book of World Records*. Joey plays midfield for me when I can't play, because of the asthma. Well, that's just how it is. Not even Larry can fix asthma.

Larry is our coach. He's the best coach in the world and because he is, the *Wild Soccer Bunch* is the best soccer team in the world. I wouldn't want to play for any other team. 'Cause there's only one thing that makes the world go round: playing for the *Wild Soccer Bunch*.

But unfortunately, right now, my world is not spinning. Seriously. There are dangers lurking everywhere and they smack you right in the face when you least expect it. We learned that the hard way. And it was serious this time. So if you're reading this book, brace yourselves. This is not a kid's book. This is real; as real as life. Dangerous and wild.

It all began when a new student joined our class.

Fabio, the wizard, the son of a Brazilian soccer star, had moved to Chicago that spring. And believe me, this guy was not our friend. This guy was the enemy; he threatened our very existence.

And then poof! Suddenly the *Wild Soccer Bunch* was no more. Suddenly the *Wild Soccer Bunch* was nothing, zilch, nada. Our opponents were none other than the *Furies,* and they snubbed us. Yes, you read that right. I'm talking about none other than the hugely successful youth club coached by real pros with ties to Major League Soccer!

How could we possibly measure up against them? We couldn't and so the *Wild Soccer Bunch* was about to be scattered to the seven winds and we'd never see each other again. We were alone.

Even our coach, Larry, had turned his back on us.

The Beginning of the End

Everything started out just beautifully. The time after spring break was simply fantastic. Roger the hero was walking on clouds. Like a curly red balloon wearing glasses with coke bottle lenses, he floated above us and told everyone he met the story of our victory.

"Dude, you won't believe it," Roger said. "We were trailing behind – zero to seven. Really. Against those morons, the *Unbeatables*. Not only were they bigger, heavier, and wider than us, they were meaner too. You should've seen them, all wearing these painted faces, like they were going into combat. They were total freaks! But I went to get Larry, and then – WHAM! We finished them off. It was me, yes, me, who sent them to the great beyond. And I did it with my weaker left foot. BAM!"

Whenever Roger said "BAM!" we'd laugh. We let him tell the story, although anyone who is anyone knows he doesn't have a weaker foot. Stands to reason, if you have a weaker foot, you must have a stronger foot, too, and Roger sure doesn't. No way. But who cares; the rest was true and we felt fantastic! We had beaten the *Unbeatables* and protected our field from that army of jellyfish. But what was even more important: we had transformed ourselves. We were no longer just a bunch of kids kicking a soccer ball around; we were a real team. A soccer team. We had grown. We were more mature. We were inseparable. And we thought it would last forever.

But if you were to ask me today what I thought about all this, I'd say this was the beginning of the end. We just didn't know it yet. We were blind, dreaming like children, resting on our laurels.

First we had to share Alex's punishment. He had been grounded for twenty days. Twenty days, are you kidding?! Imagine what that means to a nine-year-old boy. I'll tell you what it means. It's a life sentence. Worse. Alex had blasted two mid-size holes into the living room windows of his fancy home at One Woodlawn Avenue, first with a soccer ball and then with a globe. It didn't help that the globe landed on his father's head.

Although we all thought it was funny, Alex's father saw things in a slightly more serious light. You know, he's a banker and not a member of the *Wild Soccer Bunch,* and at a bank, blasting a hole in a window carries a life sentence. No ifs, ands, or buts. So in our minds, the only thing we could do was to stick together … and share Alex's sentence.

Twenty days divided by ten, that makes two days each. Two days seemed totally doable. But to Danny, who hates being grounded more than anything, two days were two days too many. And since Danny always has a plan when things are tight and desperate, he came up with a plan this time too.

Right after school on the first day after spring break, the ten of us went to Alex's house at fancy One Woodlawn Avenue. The ten of us marched right past Alex's dumbstruck mother. She had rarely seen so many kids in one place, let alone anything like the *Wild Soccer Bunch*. The ten of us greeted her politely, looked into her stone face, hoping she'd blink first. She didn't. So we stormed up the polished stairs, turning them dull as we clobbered them with our feet, and disappeared into the kids' room.

The Barbie doll house that belonged to Alex's sister was still in there, but that didn't bother us. Danny put the Barbie dolls into the trashcan and handed two pillows to Julia, Alex's whining sister. Then he explained what a cheerleader does. In the meantime, we transformed the Barbie doll house into a soccer stadium, and began our tournament. It wasn't a real tournament, though. The idea was to score as many goals as possible. Because according to Danny's plan, Julia had to dance and cheerlead with each and every goal.

At first she didn't think this was fun. She cried and whined and only used the pillows to wipe her nose. But Danny was a very patient teacher. He explained over and over again what she had to do to be a cheerleader. And finally Julia got the hang of it. She tossed the pillows in the air, skipping and dancing and spinning in circles.

She skipped and danced higher and higher, wilder and wilder, and finally didn't just skip anymore. She leapt up onto the bed, using the bounce of the mattress to trampoline back down to the ground with a thud.

BAM! Julia laughed and laughed, but on the floor below us, the ceiling shook. BAM! Exactly the way Danny planned it...

BAM! The ceiling shook again. CLINK! The crystal chandelier quivered above the dining room table, where Alex's father sat trying to read his newspaper. BAM! He was disturbed. CLINK! His tightly-wound nerves started to unravel. It was just a matter of time before he would explode. Again, Danny's brilliant plan.

Finally, when Alex's father couldn't take it anymore, he leapt to his feet and stormed up the stairs. In a nanosecond he stood in the doorway to the kids' room, with every intention of prolonging his son's punishment.

"Gentlemen, I think this is...!" He was about to bite our heads off, when suddenly he lost the ability to speak. There we were, sitting quietly on the ground, innocently looking up at him. Only Julia was bouncing up and down like mad, screeching at the top of her lungs: "*Wild Soccer Bunch* on the roll! C'mon let's see another goal!"

Alex's father just stood there like a hatchet man who'd swallowed his hatchet so he wouldn't scare his favorite daughter. He could never be angry with *Julia,* and that's exactly what Danny had counted on.

"Isn't she cute?" Danny grinned at Alex's father. "Mr. Alexander, we just couldn't make her stop, she was so into it."

Alex's father narrowed his eyes and panned from his daughter to Danny. Danny remained calm.

"Maybe *you* have the heart to make her stop, Mr. Alexander!" Danny said, encouragingly. "Her jumping is really starting to annoy us." Julia heard this and froze, then began to sob.

"Oh no! That's mean! They are so mean, Daddy!" She wrapped her little arms around her father's legs. He was ready to do anything. He wanted to kill Danny, but his weapon, the hatchet, was still stuck in his throat.

Danny took a deep breath.

"You see, Mr. Alexander!" he sighed. "We didn't want your daughter to whine like that."

It was dead quiet all of the sudden. For a moment, the quiet even swallowed Julia's whining. Then Alex's father's voice worked its way up past the hatchet, and we heard a gurgling: "Out!" he screamed.

"Excuse me?" Danny asked politely.

"Out!" this time the voice was clear.

"But we are grounded, sir!" Danny shot back. Alex's father didn't want to hear any of that. He spat out his hatchet.

"Out! All of you! You are *not grounded!!*" he ordered unmistakably.

A moment later we stormed out of the house, down the street and we ran on and on until we were out of earshot. Then we burst into laughter.

We laughed for at least half an hour. When we couldn't laugh anymore, we continued on to our original destination – our soccer field and Larry's food stand.

If you remember, the *Unbeatables* destroyed the

stand, and we were left to fix it. Well, actually the *Unbeatables* were supposed to fix it. But Mickey the bulldozer, Humungous, Octopus, Kong, and all those other morons didn't even think of keeping their end of the deal. So, because we could not turn our backs on Larry, we had to do it ourselves.

The next few days and weeks were worry free, real fun and simply fantastic. We fixed the stand, played soccer, and during the breaks, we listened to Larry tell us about past soccer wizards, the likes of Cantona, Zinedine Zidane, Van Basten, and the Brazilian Ronaldo. We closed our eyes and dreamed of being professional soccer players in the MLS. We dreamed of playing in the World Cup! We imagined great soccer stadiums, seats packed, audiences cheering for us as we'd compete with the best teams in the world! Oh yeah! Each and every one of us dreamed that dream, and each and every one of us believed that dream would come true. We truly believed we were close. But in closing our eyes to dream, we couldn't see what was real any more.

Remember, I told you, it was the beginning of the end. Even Roger, who was walking on clouds above us like a red balloon, telling everyone the story of our victory, slowly lost air. The story of our victory became stale eventually, and even Larry started yawning when he heard it.

Once he asked us if an Apache warrior without a warpath was still a warrior, and we looked at him as if he had asked us to play miniature golf on Mars. Then he wanted to know what we'd think of Luke Skywalker if he were hiding from Darth Vader, and we laughed at him, saying Luke Skywalker would never hide. And then he asked us if the *Chicago Fire* or *Colorado Rapids* would still exist if Major League Soccer had been abolished.

We had no idea what he was talking about. They were weird questions and we just didn't get it. We didn't *want* to get it and that's why we ran straight into our greatest danger yet. A danger that threatened our very existence, destroyed our dreams, and took from us everything we cared about.

Fabio

It was the day after Memorial Day when danger showed its face for the very first time. The first day of school after a long weekend is bad enough, I think. But to top it all off, I had been coughing all night and overslept. You can imagine I wasn't exactly in a good mood. I was late for school, and when I finally arrived, I was still a little out of it. Still in a daze, I walked into the classroom and straight to my seat. Then, I froze in my tracks.

The chair between Kevin and Danny, *my* chair, was taken. I was stunned. I stared at the boy. Then I heard the teacher's voice: "Students, Fabio is from Brazil. His father works here. He's playing for the *Chicago Fire* this season."

An excited murmur made its way around the classroom. Kevin, Julian, and Danny stared at the boy in my chair, awestruck.

"Wow!" they all shouted, and Kevin and Danny high fived each other. "Dude! What'd I tell you?" Danny laughed enthusiastically. "He's the son of a soccer God!"

Fabio smiled proudly when he heard this. Nobody noticed me. Even the teacher didn't seem to notice that I was standing in the aisle without a place to sit.

"I knew you would enjoy hearing this," the teacher smiled. "But I suggest you discuss the important things in life, like soccer, during recess."

Then he wrote the word *Brazil* on the board.

"Let's talk about Brazil," he said in that special tone teachers use to make offers you cannot refuse. I was not at all in the mood to talk about Brazil. But how was the teacher supposed to know that? He didn't even see me!

"Who knows anything about Fabio's home country?" the teacher asked and turned around to face us. "I mean, except for the fact that they play soccer there."

Our teacher smiled into our silence. Nobody had listened. That is, nobody but me.

"Apparently, in Brazil, people sit on the floor," I hissed like a snake.

Now everyone noticed me.

I was standing in the aisle. Fabio furrowed his brow with obvious hostility and eyeballed me up and down. Our teacher didn't appreciate my remark either.

"Oh, good morning, Diego," he said. "Would you mind explaining what you mean?"

"No problem!" I answered, still hissing. "It looks to me like they don't have enough chairs in Brazil. Or else Fabio wouldn't have stolen mine."

"Oh," the teacher said again, finally realizing what was bothering me. He looked at Kevin and Danny, and then at Fabio sitting between them on my seat. "I was under the impression you had already worked this out with Diego."

Caught red-handed, Kevin and Danny fussed with their t-shirts.

"Now I understand," the teacher nodded. "I recommend you clear this up during recess. Until then, Diego, please take a seat next to Roger."

Of course I heard. I have *20-20* hearing. I shot an angry glance at Kevin and Danny, then I walked towards the other chair. I was about to sit down, when Fabio raced from my chair and sat down in the one next to Roger, leaving my seat empty.

"Hello Diego," he said politely. "You *are* Diego the tornado, right?" he smiled. "Sorry about the chair thing."

I stared at him for a moment. Ignoring his smile, I walked back to my own seat between Kevin and Danny.

"Dude, what's up?" Kevin whispered. "We thought you were sick."

"Yeah, man!" Danny sighed. "And we're really sorry. I swear, Diego."

But I didn't give a rip about their apologies. I opened my books and stared at the boring pictures.

"Fabio's cool, Diego," Julian said from the row behind me, trying to ease the tension. "He said he wants to practice with us today. Isn't that cool?"

"Cool?" I hissed through clenched teeth. "Who exactly is it that's coming for practice? Fabio or his father?"

I glared at Fabio.

"I mean, it's your father who's the soccer pro, right? So how do we know you can even play?"

Fabio scowled at me, and then looked to Kevin and Danny.

"Look, that's not important!" Roger chimed in. "Fabio is a good guy. He's new. He doesn't have any friends."

"So what," I snarled. "Go ahead and play with him then."

That put a lid on it. Even the teacher was speechless and forgot to start the lesson.

"I'm sorry," Kevin said to Fabio. "Diego isn't always like this. He's worried we're going to replace him with you. Am I right?" he said, staring straight at me.

That hit home. Hard. But I wouldn't admit it. I ignored him and stared out the window. "You can kiss my shin-guards!" I grumbled. "Fabio is no friend of mine. He is not nice or cool. He's stuck-up and arrogant. You'll see." Yes, that's what I thought then. I was sure of it. And it didn't take long before everyone knew I was right.

Fabio, the Wizard

When I arrived on the field that afternoon, everyone else was already there. Everyone but Fabio. They were sitting in a circle around Larry, crooning about the Brazilian wonder child. Joey and Kyle, who attend different schools than the rest of us, didn't know Fabio yet and couldn't believe their ears.

"Wow!" Joey murmured. "Ribaldo's son? You serious?"

Kyle whistled.

"If he plays only half as well as his old man, he's a God."

I rolled my eyes.

"A God? Give me a break. Why is he hiding then?"

The others looked at me in surprise and even Larry scowled.

"I bet he doesn't show," I spat. "He won't dare. He's scared because he's not all that good."

At that very moment someone tapped my shoulder.

"Hello, Diego!" Fabio said, walked past me and sat down with the others. He was greeted enthusiastically.

"Hey, Fabio!"

"Glad you could make it!"

"Dude, your jersey looks cool."

"What kind of shoes are those?"

Fabio wore the jersey of the Brazilian national team and his shoes were golden. They almost blinded you.

"My father gave them to me," he said proudly.

'What a loser! Nothin' but a show-off!' I thought, rolling my eyes.

But the others obviously didn't think so. Even Larry got up, something he had never done for any of us, and extended his hand to Fabio.

"You're Fabio," he said, just as my ball hit him in the chest.

"What are we waiting for?" I demanded, glaring at everyone. "I'm here to practice."

Larry's eyes wandered from me to Fabio. He pushed his cap far back on his head and scratched his forehead. He always did that when he had to think hard.

"I see. Okay. Let's play four against two. The four outside are Danny, Kevin, Fabio and Diego. Roger and I play in the center."

I clenched my fist and pressed my lips together. This was not what I had in mind.

Fabio and I on the same team? I sure didn't

appreciate that. But Larry's glance didn't allow any room for arguing.

"Okay. Fine!" I sulked. "How many passes?"

"Seven!" Larry announced. "If you can manage seven passes without Roger or me getting to the ball, you get a point. Otherwise we do, and three points win."

I looked at Fabio, my enemy.

"Seven passes, you hear?"

"Yes, seven," he nodded. "Got it."

"Good," I shot back and picked up the ball. "And just so we're clear, Fabio, the center has never won."

I ran out to the field, dropped the ball and waited for the others to take position. Kevin, Danny, Fabio and I made a circle about twenty feet apart from each other. Roger and Larry took position in the middle. The first pass was easy, but then things heated up. Larry and Roger charged towards us. Winning would take fast and precise passes. But I didn't want to win. I wanted to lose, and I wanted it to be Fabio's fault. So I directed the first pass to him. I played it hard and low. I knew that was against the rules but I wanted him to lose the ball the first time he tried. 'Losing the ball to Roger would seal the deal,' I thought. Fabio would be humiliated and I'd keep my spot on the team.

They'd see that I didn't give up that easily. Everything

went according to plan. Roger saw my pass and fully expected what I expected. No way could anyone stop that ball. That's why Roger threw himself onto Fabio to catch the ricochet. But Roger straddled into nothing. Fabio plucked the ball from the air with his big toe as if he had a lasso, lifted it on his thighs, played over Roger's head, took it with his left foot and, although Larry was charging him, played it past him to Danny.

But neither Danny nor Kevin moved. They were as amazed as I was.

"Tight!" Roger exclaimed. "That was really wild!"

"No! That was magic!" Danny shouted, ran towards the ball and passed to Kevin.

"Three!" he counted out loud.

Kevin took the ball while I ran to a free spot.

"Here!" I shouted, but Kevin shot a pass back to Danny, who passed to Fabio, although I had shouted "here" yet again, and was completely free and unguarded.

"Five!" Danny and Kevin shouted at the same time. Fabio wasn't free and unguarded. He stood right in between Larry and Roger and they charged him immediately. Fabio had less room than a postage stamp to move on, but he stayed calm. He stepped on the ball, pushed his butt back, turned in a quarter circle, shouted "Danny, watch out!" tossed the ball straight in the air and headed it back to me.

"Six!" he shouted. "Diego, come on, time for number 7!"

But I didn't move. My jaw dropped to the floor. I was furious. I couldn't and wouldn't admit I was wrong about Fabio. The last thing I wanted was for him to be a great soccer player.

"Come on, Diego, pass the ball!" Danny shouted. I looked at him. Then I looked for the ball, but I just couldn't find it.

"You blind or something!?" Kevin exploded. "Look!"

I looked. The ball was at my feet. I blushed, that's how mortified I was. I lifted my foot. Kevin was free. The seventh pass should have been child's play. That's when Roger slid into my shot.

"One to zero for the center!" he shouted triumphantly, and Danny and Kevin shook their heads in disbelief.

"Diego, what's the matter with you?"

I looked at Larry, pleading for help, but he didn't come to my rescue. He just looked back at me. But I couldn't do or say anything. I was humiliated. Instead of Fabio, I had been the one to lose the ball to Roger, and that made me even more furious. But I was no longer angry with Fabio, I was angry with myself.

"Come on! Let's go on!" I sulked, took the ball and this time I played a clean pass to Kevin.

"One!" I gathered some courage, but the pass was too short.

"Awww!" Kevin complained, but he got to the ball just before Roger did, and passed it to Danny, who played it back to Kevin, who gunned it to Fabio.

"Four!" I shouted loudly.

The pass was imprecise. Larry charged and I was sure he'd catch it. But Fabio slid into the ball before Larry could get there, picked it up with his left foot and tipped it gently towards me with his right.

'Impossible!' I thought and stopped the ball with my right. 'No mistakes now,' I pleaded with myself. I placed the ball so I could kick it with my right, but I had to double step to do so and that took time. Roger reached the ball before me.

"Two zero for the center!" he shouted. All I wanted was a hole in the ground to hide in.

That's when Fabio came over to me.

"Diego?" he asked politely. "Can I tell you something?"

I glared at him. "And what would that be?"

Fabio met my gaze. "I usually stop the ball with my weaker foot so I can play it with my stronger foot right away. No double steps that way."

He put the ball at his feet with his left and then quickly passed it to me with his right.

"You see?" he smiled, but I just stared at him. 'What is he babbling about, a weaker foot?' I thought. 'The way he plays he has *five strong* feet.'

I was upset. Fabio took the ball.

"This is serious now!" he shouted. "We'll have to score the next three points in a row."

I swallowed anxiously. The ball rolled towards Kevin,

who played a quick pass to Danny. Then the pass came to me. 'I have to make it,' I thought, 'at any cost,' but then I saw Roger and Larry charging towards me. My right foot touched the ball automatically. 'No, that's wrong,' I thought and pulled my leg back. Big mistake! The ball rolled right through my legs. I couldn't believe it. I turned around as quickly as possible, pushed my body between the ball and Roger, blocked him, stopped the ball with my left and passed to Fabio with my right.

"Wow!" he said. "That was fantastic!"

I beamed and shouted: "Five!" I was back in the groove.

After that everything was easy. Kevin and Danny made the next two points and the score was two to two. The next point would decide the match. Kevin started. He cut to Fabio, who passed the ball to me. Everything worked beautifully. Roger slid into nothing again and again, and after the fifth time he complained.

"It's not fair!" he shouted. "Fabio is way too good!"

Larry reacted differently. He turned his game up a notch and showed us what he had. We were stunned. We had never seen him play like that. Larry was even better than Fabio, despite his lame leg. It took quite an effort to make the sixth pass. One more pass and we would have won. But it wasn't that easy. Fabio had the

ball, but Larry cornered him. Fabio had to give it his all
to get the ball to me. But the pass was too hard and too
low. I couldn't take it with my foot. I looked around.
Roger towered behind me, confident of certain victory.
That's when I threw myself onto the ball and headed it
to Kevin. He stopped the pass with his chest.

"Alright! That's seven!" he shouted. "We did it!"

"That was fantastic, Diego!" Danny added.

But I was on the ground, looking up at Fabio.

"Thanks!" I said to him.

"What for?" Fabio shrugged his shoulders, grinning.
Then he reached out his hand and helped me up.

"Without you," he said, "I would have messed it up."

I couldn't believe he said that.

Then we all walked off the field to the stand. Larry sprang for a round of lemonades and we sat down in the grass around Fabio. Fabio told us about the beaches in Brazil and about his friends. He told us how sad he was when he had to leave, and how glad he was to have met us. Then he paused and looked at his golden shoes for a long time, suddenly uncomfortable.

"I'd really like to play with you," he hesitated. "Is that what you want, too?"

"Does the deer live in the woods?" Danny beamed.

"Of course we do!" the others shouted. "What kind of question is that?"

But then Fabio looked up from his shoes, directly at me.

"What about you, Diego?" his voice was barely audible. "Do you want that, too?"

I blushed, fighting the lump in my throat. I could see that Fabio was anxious.

"Dude!" I swallowed. "More than anything!"

I grinned and we high-fived. My anger and jealousy had vanished. At that moment, I would have done anything for him. And if someone had told me what was going to happen the next day, I would have called them a liar.

Diego is Right

The next morning at school, we were all waiting for
Fabio. We felt 10-feet-tall and like 12-year-olds. We
were a real soccer team with a real Brazilian on the
team, just like the MLS. And we knew that if you play
in the MLS, you're really cool. You're no longer afraid of
anyone, not even Mickey the bulldozer.

Suddenly, that's who appeared right before us, his

Darth Vader shirt desperately trying to keep his fat bulges from exploding all over the playground. When he breathed, he sounded like a seal snoring, and his beady little eyes beamed like hot lasers from the fatty folds of his face, gunning us up and down. As usual, he picked on the weakest of the bunch. Me.

"Out of my way, Asthma!" he hissed. Right behind him stood Octopus, Kong, the monumental creature from the prairies of Mongolia, and the Grim Reaper, wearing the usual chains around his neck.

I swallowed, expecting an asthma attack. Asthma attacks and Mickey the bulldozer always seem to go together. But that day my breathing stayed calm. I watched myself, as if I was dreaming.

"What do you want?" I asked the monster jellyfish. "In case you didn't notice, this is a school, not the zoo!"

Mickey squinted. He didn't expect that to come out of my mouth and therefore couldn't think of anything to say.

"In case you didn't know, schools are for intelligent creatures who walk upright," I explained, not believing what I was saying. This was the kind of stuff Kevin and Danny would say. Now I know why. It was fun.

"Do you really think," I continued, "you belong to that species?"

The bulldozer's beady eyes darted back and forth like

crazy, that's how much his small brain had to work. He was suffering mental overload.

"Monsters like you belong in the zoo. You get what I'm saying?" I needled him, totally oblivious to the danger I was in.

The bulldozer's face swelled and lit up from the inside like a lava lamp. His beady eyes drilled holes into me. The Darth Vader shirt rippled, like the ground during an earthquake, as he tried to grab me with his huge meaty hands. I ducked, but I wasn't quick enough. He grabbed me by my shirt and lifted me effortlessly off the ground. My legs dangled in the air.

"You are so dead, Asthma!" Mickey seethed into my face, his breath so bad I could see it.

But I didn't give up. I swallowed his stinking breath, grinned back, and went for the big guns. "Let me down, or I'll serve your butt to Sox for breakfast!"

Mickey froze and looked quickly around, beads of sweat forming on his massive pimply forehead. Octopus, Grim Reaper and Kong also looked for Kevin's dog with the big flapping ears.

"Where is that stupid dog?" Mickey shouted. "Where is it!?" He shook me in panic. "Asthma, I'm not kidding, where is it?"

"There!" I said. "In the parking lot, between those

cars, see him? He's coming for you, meathead. Prepare to die!"

"Where," he screamed. "I can't see him."

"He's right behind you!"

Mickey jumped three feet, then let go of me and ran like he was being chased by a T. Rex. Octopus, Grim Reaper and Kong were right on his heels.

"Run, Mickey, run!" we shouted after them. Then we screamed with laughter, because Sox wasn't nearby. In fact, he wasn't even in town. He was on vacation on the East Coast with Kevin's mother. But Mickey the bulldozer didn't know that, and that's why he ran away from the parked busses, stormed into school, and slammed the door behind him.

We laughed and laughed.

"That was tight, Diego!" Danny praised me, and we laughed until Fabio drove up in his dad's car. Talk about awesome. Giacomo Ribaldo, the Brazilian star striker, was driving the car himself. He wore his training gear, obviously on his way to the *Fire* daily training. Fabio sat in the back, looking at us.

"Hey, Fabio!" I shouted.

"Sick, dude!" Danny greeted him.

"I'd love to live that," Roger exclaimed, "Giacomo Ribaldo driving me to school!"

Julian shook his head. "And to think, Fabio just calls him 'Dad'!"

"Yes," I said impressed. "But that's some dad."

We looked over to Fabio, who pointed at us. Obviously he was telling his father about us. We were bursting with pride, and it was almost unbearable when Giacomo Ribaldo himself looked at us. It wasn't exactly a look. It was more of a glare. Something was wrong. Then he shook his head. Fabio tried saying something, but it looked like his father cut him off. The matter was closed. Fabio remained seated, but then his father obviously ordered him to get out of the car, and he obeyed.

"Hey, Fabio!" we shouted. "What's up?" Fabio looked back at his father, but there was no reaction.

"Nothing!" he said, and marched right past us.

"Fabio," I shouted. "Wait!"

But Fabio walked straight into the building. We watched him until he disappeared inside. His dad watched him too. Then he drove off, without even a look our way.

I was confused and angry. "Nothing," I imitated Fabio's answer, "Right! I've heard that before. You know? I don't believe him. Something is up."

"Right on," Danny said. "What are we waiting for?"

Actually, we weren't waiting for anything, so we ran across the playground into the building and our classroom, marched up to Fabio's seat and stood in front of him like a wall.

Fabio glanced at us briefly. Then he fumbled with his backpack.

"What's up?" I asked. "Not talking to us anymore?"

Fabio shook his head. It wasn't an answer that came from someone who decided on something, it was more an embarrassed, humiliated twitch.

"Any reason why not?"

Fabio looked at me, but didn't say anything.

"Come on, dude, talk to me."

"I'm too busy for this nonsense!" Fabio shot back. "I have to concentrate on school."

That's when our teacher showed up, but I didn't care.

Fabio was more important.

"What about practice?"

Fabio looked at me. Then he shrugged his shoulders arrogantly. "Practice? What's the point? I can't learn anything from you guys anyway."

His gaze was cold, only his eyes glistened a bit, as if one or two tears had lost their way. But we couldn't see that. We were too angry and too disappointed. I had been right after all. Fabio was not our friend. He was just messing with us, like we were some minor distraction.

Later, we sat on the field, sad, not in the mood for practice at all. Our lemonade was getting warm, and we were playing around in the grass with sticks.

"He's as arrogant as his father!" said Danny, as he finished his report to Larry.

"I think I know what's going on here," Kyle said, "It's not Fabio at all. It's his dad."

"I don't know." I shook my head. "A father wouldn't do something like that."

"That's what you think," Kyle responded. "Mine sure does. I tell you, he'll do anything to keep me from playing soccer."

"Okay so maybe yours doesn't care much for soccer," Kevin responded, "but Fabio's father is Giacomo Ribaldo. He doesn't exactly play Monopoly for a living!"

"Right," Kyle mumbled. "But why? I don't get it. Yesterday Fabio was playing on our team. He was totally cool."

"Very true," Larry said. "And that's why maybe the problem isn't Fabio or Ribaldo. Maybe the problem is you."

"What?!" Kevin burst out angrily. "Now you're not making any sense. What did *we* do?" We stared at Larry, hoping this was another lesson about Apache warriors without a warpath, Luke Skywalker, and abolishing Major League Soccer. But Larry was serious, more serious than he'd ever been before.

"I think it's time you understand what's really going on here," he said. "And if you don't get it, then go to Fabio and Ribaldo's house. I'm sure they'll be happy to explain it to you. I'll eat my hat if they don't."

We stared at him.

"Ribaldo's house?" I asked.

"You want us to go to Giacomo Ribaldo's house?" Danny asked. "Are you serious?"

"You want the truth, don't you?"

"OMG!" Roger sighed.

"Maybe we will pay him a visit," I challenged him.

"Wait a minute," Roger said. "I bet the house is secured and gated and their yard is crawling with more bodyguards than fruit flies."

"And they have guns!" Josh added. Then he shot an imaginary gun and fell to the ground, gurgling as if shot to death.

"We can't just show up on his doorstep," Tyler explained. "Giacomo Ribaldo is a celebrity. A *real* soccer star."

"Correct," Larry nodded. "And exactly what you all want to be some day. Right?"

We couldn't disagree.

"So what are you waiting for?"

We stood up hesitantly. A thundercloud darkened the sun, and I looked down at Josh, still lying in the grass as if he were dead. He was only playing, of course, but I couldn't help feeling that soon all of us would be lying on the ground like that. Defeated. Except in our case, it wouldn't be a game. It would be real.

At Heaven's Gate

Giacomo Ribaldo lived on a street called Heaven's Gate. We'd always heard about this area, but none of us had ever been anywhere near it. And now we were marching right up to it. We expected to see castles floating in the clouds. Instead, the very moment we stepped onto the street, the castles dropped from heaven and plunked down their sky-high walls right in front of us. There were no houses, only huge gates, silently warning us: 'What do you want? You have no business here.'

If you ask me, the gates were right. But we knew Fabio's address, and so we approached one of the iron gates anyway.

It said "9," which was Giacomo Ribaldo's number. It was also Fernando Torres's number, the Spanish soccer striker who happened to be Kevin's idol. It was Mia Hamm's number, the greatest American female soccer player of all time. But that number was the only thing that welcomed us.

We stood in front of the towering gate, unsure of what to do. Thunderclouds hung directly on top of us, like a message from above. Danny nervously whistled a tune: "Knocking on Heaven's Door." He said this was what his father did every time he was afraid. Danny was still whistling as he rang the bell.

Nothing happened for what seemed like an eternity. Then a voice answered in Portuguese. That's the language they speak in Brazil, we knew that much. But we didn't understand a word.

"Excuse us!" Danny stammered and scratched his head. "We'd like to see Fabio?"

The speaker croaked back something, as if Danny had asked to marry Fabio. Then it was quiet. We were about to leave when the buzzer startled us. One wing of the dark iron gate swung open, and beyond it, we could see the house in the mist.

Wow! Compared to this house, Alex's fancy home on One Woodlawn Avenue was a tool shed and Kyle's father's mansion was a creaky old boat house. This was a castle and the garden surrounding it was not a garden, it was a park.

Slowly, knees buckling, we slid through the gate. The path to the house was as long as the highway to heaven. But this heaven was dark and grey. Lightning lit up the clouds and thunderclaps disturbed the peace. Suddenly we remembered our fingernails. We tried to clean them with our teeth and used spit to wipe the dirt from our faces.

"What do you want with Fabio?" a frosty voice greeted us.

We shuddered. One last time the low sun broke through the clouds, blinding us as we looked around. But then we saw them. They stood near us on the terrace. Giacomo Ribaldo, the soccer star, had his arm around Fabio's shoulders.

"Oh, ah, we wanted to..." Danny stammered. "We wanted to... well, we didn't mean to bother you." He flashed his irresistible smile, but it didn't work at all.

"Good," Giacomo Ribaldo nodded. "Anything else?" He shot a threatening glance our way.

"Well actually w-we want Fabio to play on our team," Tyler spat it out quickly. The Brazilian soccer star squinted. So I added quickly: "He's our friend."

I looked at Fabio: "Am I right?"

But Fabio didn't meet my gaze.

"Is that what you want, son?" Giacomo Ribaldo asked drippingly. "Look at me!" he added sternly.

Fabio looked directly into his father's eyes. He hesitated, I could see it in his eyes, clear as day, but then he shook his head.

I couldn't believe it.

"Good. That's good, son" Giacomo Ribaldo said and turned towards us. "There you go. You have your answer. Good day."

We stayed put.

"He's not going to play soccer?" I asked softly.

The Brazilian star laughed. "He'll play. But not with you. My son will play with a club team – the *Furies*. Someday, Fabio will *be* somebody."

"We're going to be somebody too. We're going to be professionals!" Kevin dared to say.

Giacomo Ribaldo looked at him, and laughed even louder.

"Sure. If you've got what it takes."

Kevin glared at him: "Was that supposed to be an insult?"

We twitched. Even Fabio held his breath. But Giacomo Ribaldo seemed impressed. His smile faded.

"Not at all," he said coldly. "But if you really want to be a soccer pro, I wouldn't waste my time with *this* team."

His eyes wandered from Kevin to Roger to me. I have to admit I was so upset that my asthma caught up with me. But Kevin is different. He'll rise to any challenge.

"It's not a waste of time to play with this team," he shot back, squinting at Ribaldo. "You know why? Because this is the best team in the world!"

For the tiniest moment Giacomo Ribaldo was speechless. Kevin looked at Fabio.

"I hope you heard me, Fabio," Kevin said with pride.

Fabio returned his gaze, and I thought he might agree, but then his father stopped him short.

"Don't be ridiculous!" he said coldly. "This is no team. You are nothing but a bunch of boys kicking a ball around, dreaming the dream every little boy in the world dreams. To become a real player, like me."

Lightning shot from the clouds, and thunder followed

immediately afterwards.

Then it was quiet. We stood there, paralyzed, as if an evil sorcerer had turned us to stone.

Only Tyler still moved. He shook his head slowly: "Sorry. That's not what I'm dreaming!" he said with resolve, looking Fabio directly in the eye. "Nobody here wants to be like you, except you."

Fabio held Tyler's gaze. Then he freed himself from his father's embrace and ran back into the house. His father looked after him, surprised.

"That goes for the rest of us," Danny confirmed as lightning and thunder cracked down upon us.

Giacomo Ribaldo looked at us one more time. It was an arch gaze none of us could stand. We were mortified, and so we ran. We ran back out into the street and kept running until we reached the soccer field. There, we hoped we'd be able to shake that look he gave us.

But we were not that lucky. Larry was waiting for us.

It's All Over

Larry was closing up his stand, carrying the newspapers into the wooden shed.

"So? What did he say?" he asked casually as if he was talking about the weather. But the question

wasn't casual at all, because when he came out of his shed, he looked at us as if he knew everything. Even worse. Larry's' glance was like Ribaldo's: merciless and humiliating.

As we stood there, out of breath, angry, the first rain drops hitting our faces, the realization struck us like a thunderstorm. Giacomo Ribaldo was right. We were no soccer team. None of us had what it takes to become a soccer pro. Our dreams burst like soap bubbles in the piercing rain. And let me tell you something: if you don't have a dream, you don't have anything.

"So?" Larry asked. "Now what?"

We looked at him, desperate and angry. For the first time in a long time, we didn't know what to do. What kind of question was that anyway? Wasn't that *his* job? He was our coach. He was supposed to tell us what to do. But Larry didn't even consider it. He limped to the stand and locked up the windows and the door. Kevin clenched his fists.

"Okay, there's only one thing we can do," he said. "We play the *Furies!*" he shouted. "We'll show that snob Ribaldo. We'll kick the *Furies* straight to the moon, right along with his sniveling little son, Fabio."

Larry looked at Kevin.

"Are you saying what I think you're saying?" he asked.

"Read my lips," Kevin hissed. "Yes."

Larry nodded. "Great idea, Kevin."

But then he sighed.

"Too bad the *Furies* won't accept the challenge. They'll laugh you right out of town. Yep, that's what they'll do, unless..."

He thought for a moment, but then he shook his head.

"No, I don't think it'll work. It's over. Go home!"

Larry limped to his beat-up motorcycle and unlocked it.

"Oh, and before I forget to tell you, practice is over, too, and not just for today. The soccer field is off limits to you. I don't want to see any of you ever again. Is that clear?"

He looked at us one last time.

"And if you don't know what I mean, just take a look in the mirror. The *Wild Soccer Bunch* I knew... is history."

He floored it and drove off.

We stood like statues in the pouring rain. We couldn't believe it. One by one we sat down on the grass, thunderstruck. I knew if we stayed we would all catch pneumonia, but I didn't care. I remembered Josh and the feeling I had when he was lying in the grass playing dead. I could hear Ribaldo's laugh and his words, "If you really want to be a soccer pro, you shouldn't waste your time with this team." Then I heard Larry, "I don't want to see any of you ever again. The *Wild Soccer Bunch* is history."

And I saw Fabio shake his head again and again when asked if he'd want to be our friend.

None of us could believe it. Even Kevin bit his lips, wiping a drop of water from his face as if it was a tear. The *Wild Soccer Bunch* was history.

What were we going to do? We were clueless, so we just sat there in the rain getting wetter and wetter, until the fierce cold finally got to us. Then we walked home. Each of us by himself. Alone.

Scattered in the Wind

My mother got real scared when she saw me. I stood
in the kitchen, shaking from the cold, sopping wet,
not saying a word. I couldn't. I was waiting for her
to get angry with me. "Diego, are you crazy? Are you
trying to catch your death of cold? I thought you were
a responsible young man. I must have been wrong. No
more soccer for you. Is that clear?"

That is what I was waiting for. Hoping for, actually.
My body was numb and my head was wrapped in cotton
balls. I was stuck in a nightmare and I was hoping
someone would wake me up.

But my mother didn't say anything. She just looked at
me. She looked at me like I'd been skinned, quartered,
and shot by seven deadly arrows. Then she took me
in her arms and put me in the bathtub. And after that
she made me some hot chocolate. She behaved like
an angel. She took care of me as if I was a seriously
wounded knight who had won the tournament. But I
wasn't wounded. I was also no knight and I sure hadn't

fought in a tournament. I was a loser, with a big L on my forehead. I had been beaten without a fight. I had lost everything: Larry, our coach; the soccer field; and the center of the world, my friends in the *Wild Soccer Bunch*. And worst of all, soccer, which was everything to me.

That's why my mother's care didn't help one bit. Okay so she made sure I didn't catch pneumonia or a cold, but I read that as pity. Pity? Give me a break! Can you believe it?

In such an important moment of my life, pity was the worst thing that could happen to me. I needed something different. I needed someone who would kick my butt; someone who would tell me I should take my head out of the sand; someone who would take away my fear and give me back my courage; someone who would tell me what to do to get my pride and my dreams back. I needed my dad. But he was long gone. All I had was my mother, and she felt pity. Bummer! So that's why I refused to talk to her that first night and kept my lips zipped for the next few days. Not a word.

Things weren't much different for the other guys in the *Wild Soccer Bunch*. From one day to the next our world had changed, as if a meteor had swooped down from space and destroyed everything. Even the climate had changed. At least that's what it felt like. Summer turned to fall. The rain poured down incessantly from dark clouds hanging above the trees like black sulfur. We couldn't look each other in the eye. We just stared at our feet.

We didn't even talk to each other at school. I sat between Danny and Kevin and never said a word. Behind us, Julian and Roger were silent as well. We were so quiet even the teacher noticed. Fabio looked worried. But we didn't say anything to our teacher, and we totally ignored Fabio. He was no longer a part of us.

After school we went home. We didn't want to be with each other. Kevin didn't even want to see Kyle, and Julian didn't want to see Josh.

On 44 Dearborn Street, Danny tossed his Legos against the wall and helped his mother iron clothes. He grabbed the folded laundry, put it in a basket, and then put it all away. This was a first for him. His mother was in shock. She just stood there and stared at her son, mesmerized, while she ironed, never noticing when the dress she was ironing caught fire on the ironing board.

"Mom!" Danny yelled, as he pulled the iron off the dress and poured a glass of water on the flames. "What's *up* with you?"

"What's up with *you*?" She shot back. "Why aren't

you on the soccer field?" Danny jumped from one leg to the next, tried to smile his irresistible smile, but she remained stoic, so for the second time in his life, it didn't work. Nothing was working, so he quickly and angrily turned on his heel and went to his room.

"You don't get it!" he yelled and banged the door shut behind him.

In the house across the street, Julian and Josh's mother came home from work. She put her key in the lock. She didn't notice the small puddles of water slowly seeping out from under the door. But when she opened the door, she was hit by a wall of water that rushed past her, almost knocking her down. The water in the kitchen was at least five inches high, and standing smack dab in the middle of the flood was her son Julian, holding a brush.

"Back already?" he asked, nonchalantly. "We were going to surprise you."

His mother looked from her son to her feet, which were covered in water up to her ankles. Then she saw the source of the flood: the bathroom. With all the resolve she could muster she walked towards the bathroom and banged at the locked door until Julian handed her the key.

"We were fighting," he grinned.

"So you locked your brother in the bathroom?"

"Right, when he wasn't looking," Julian nodded matter-of-factly. "But we are fine now. Josh is cleaning up."

Julian's mother opened the door. The entire bathroom was full of soap bubbles, floor to ceiling.

"Josh!" she shouted as a second flood smashed against her on its way to the kitchen. The flood was so strong this time she lost her balance and landed on her rear.

As the wall of soap bubbles crashed through, her younger son was revealed behind it. He stood on the toilet, cleaning the window above it on his tiptoes.

"Hi Mom!" he greeted her. "We're cleaning up. Great, huh?"

Josh grinned like the Abominable Snowman, covered in soap bubbles.

His mother just stared, incredulous. Finally, she spoke: "Cleaning up?" she asked, struggling to her feet, slipping and landing on her rear again.

"Cleaning up! Right," she sighed as Julian came over, worried.

"Are you okay, mom?" he asked softly, trying to help her up. But she would have none of it.

"Am I *okay*? Are you kidding me?" she yelled at him. "Why are you here anyway? Go to the soccer field, please!"

Julian and Josh turned to stone.

"Go on, get out!" she repeated, but Julian and Josh

just shook their heads.

"Excuse me? Are you saying what I think you're saying?"

"We can't go to the field!" Josh whispered, and Julian cast his eyes downward in disappointment. "You know, we were positive you'd ground us for at least two weeks for what we did to the bathroom."

"Get out!" she shouted.

"Maybe two weeks is too long. How about three days?" Julian pleaded, and Josh chimed in. "Yes, three days. Please Mom, that's not too much to ask, is it?"

At 58 Wilson Street, Kevin voluntarily took Sox for a walk just to kill time. Then he beat his drums so hard even the soundproof walls of the practice room in the basement couldn't soften his fury. He didn't stop until the last eardrum was burst.

Tyler, his brother who was one year older than him, sat in their room, ear plugs in place, reading the books he borrowed from the library: *Dream Professions; 50 Surefire Ways to Success; The 100 Top Professions of Our Time.* He leafed through these books without any excitement, searching for a new vocation in life. His dream to become soccer pro had burst. He had to find a new purpose in life. But the job of a top manager or a stock broker or an online advertising consultant just wouldn't cut it. These jobs would never replace what Tyler felt in his heart when winning a one-on-one fight, cutting a dream pass, or scoring an impossible goal. That's why Tyler took out his ear plugs every night, grabbed his saxophone, and went into the woods to play the blues underneath the weeping willows.

Sometimes strains of the blues reached the soccer field where Larry sat in his rocking chair beneath the umbrella that was fastened to the armrest. He was lonely and without a job since he had declared the end of practice. He didn't even have to open the stand because there were no customers. But no matter how depressed and sad Tyler's melodies were, Larry remained tough as nails and wouldn't budge. What was he waiting for? What was his plan? What did he want the *Wild Soccer Bunch* to do?

We had no clue. At his house on One Woodlawn Avenue, our pal Alex played Barbie dolls with his younger sister for three long days. Then he got up, sorted his soccer collection, made a list of his valuable items, and posted it on Craig's List. Who needs soccer balls? They were nothing but a painful reminder of the past.

Roger had been hit hardest. Roger, the hero, really *had* been our hero for a few weeks. But now he picked up the phone, called his mother's girlfriends, and asked their daughters to come by and visit. Ten minutes later they stood at his door, monsters with lace and ribbons in their hair. But Roger didn't care. He sat in a chair in the hallway and waited to be the guinea pig for make-up kits and curling irons.

That's how bad things got, three days into the eternal rain; three days after our visit to Heaven's Gate Number 9; three days after Giacomo Ribaldo's biting ridicule, Fabio's snubbing our friendship and Larry's refusal to coach us. On that third day it was clear: The *Wild Soccer Bunch* was history.

What I had announced early in the story as the beginning of the end had overwhelmed us, flattened us, and scattered us to the seven winds. We had rested on our laurels for too long. We had been lying in the sun, dreaming, for too long. But I tell you, dreaming does not make a dream come true. You have to fight for a dream, and honestly, we were just too scared. Of course we wanted to play soccer, and of course we wanted to be real soccer pros when we grew up. But we were afraid that Ribaldo was right.

Actually, it was even worse than that.

We *knew* Giacomo Ribaldo was right. Yes, he was right on the money. We were nothing. We were just a bunch of kids kicking around a soccer ball. We weren't good enough and never would be; we'd never get anywhere in the world of soccer. It was over.

The Applesauce Duel

On day four I came home from school as usual, stepped into our house, walked past my mother, tossed my backpack in the corner, sat down at the table and silently stared out the window. I didn't care that my mother had made a pile of pancakes, my favorite meal. And when she encouraged me to eat, all I did was roll my eyes and push the pancakes away as if they had transformed into a pot full of slimy grits.

"What's the matter, Diego?" she asked, worried. "Want to talk about it?"

I sighed and rolled my eyes again. Not again. She was just my mother. When would she get that?

I needed my father, but he wasn't here and he hadn't even called me once since they split up.

"Diego, I'm talking to you!" my mother said, reminding me she was still there.

"But I'm not talking to you!" I spat. "Leave me alone. I don't need your pity."

I wiped a tear off my face and stared out the window again.

"Hm. Okay. I get it. You disrespect your mother and you want no pity." My mother nodded and began eating her pancakes calmly. "And I won't feel sorry for you that you lost all your friends and you're never going to play soccer again. Is that about the size of it?"

"Yes!" I spat again. "You don't know anything!"

I was fuming, but my mother held my gaze. She looked at me, and saw my tears. But she didn't budge. She remained cold and merciless. She squinted. Then she put both hands on the table and took a deep breath.

"Oh boy, oh boy, oh boy!" she said with a deep voice as if she was a gunslinger in a cowboy movie, about to draw her gun. "Was that an insult, boy?"

She grabbed the spoon and held it tight, like a six-shooter.

"Fine. You better choose your weapon, then," she grumbled in a raspy voice. "Because pardner, where I come from, them's fightin' words. *Nobody* insults the *Wild Soccer Bunch*."

I looked at her as if she was nuts. But to tell you the truth, she was actually starting to look like a gunslinger.

"Cut it out, mom!" I said, embarrassed, but she brushed me off. She wasn't my mother any more. She was a gunslinger and she was merciless.

"Leave me alone," she said, imitating me in her dark gunslinger voice. "What are you—a wimp?"

That hurt. Tears shot into my eyes.

"Stop it!" I begged her.

"Too late, pardner," she rasped. "You can run, but you cannot hide."

"I'm *not* hiding!" I protested.

"Hahaha! Don't make me laugh," she mocked me again. "You're so scared you're about to jump out of your skin."

"All right, that's enough!" I threatened the gunslinger. "Stop it..."

"*You* stop it!" she cut me short, sniffing the air. "I can smell it. It smells like... self-pity. Yuck, it's gross."

"Stop it!" I yelled. "Stop it right now!"

I stared down the gunslinger, and for a brief moment, I believe I made the monster stop.

"Dang," the gunslinger swore, because she couldn't think of anything else. But then she spat and this move showed the scale of her contempt.

"You know what you are? You're a... chicken."

I couldn't breathe. You don't want to hear that coming from your own mother, even if she is a gunslinger.

"No, I'm not," I said quietly.

"You're right, you're worse. You're a wimp," she responded.

"No!" I shouted.

"Then prove it, tinhorn. Draw... or face my wrath!"

It got real quiet. The gunslinger's eyes locked on my chest. I could barely move. But I fought back. I wiped the tears from my face and took a deep breath. Then I grabbed a spoon from the table.

"You asked for it!" I said roughly, and the gunslinger nodded. Then she drew. With lightning speed, the spoon shot forward towards the applesauce. But she wasn't fast enough. I had already spooned out some applesauce and put it in my mouth.

Oh, let me tell you dear reader, it was good.

The gunslinger was surprised. "Not bad!" she murmured. This time she really was impressed. "But you know, my boy, it's much better with pancakes. Here. Catch!"

With that, the gunslinger pulled a pancake from the pile and threw it towards me like a Frisbee. I plucked it out of the air and stuffed it in my mouth.

"True!" I grinned with my mouth full. The gunslinger grinned back.

"Fine! Stuff your face, you hear, and while you do that, I'll tell you a story. Man to man."

I swallowed until my mouth was finally empty, and then I nodded: "Okay. Deal!"

The gunslinger smiled and with this smile he morphed back into my mother. I ate seven pancakes with syrup and then seven with sugar and cinnamon. But I didn't notice. I just listened to my mom weave her tale. It was the most exciting and suspenseful story I'd ever heard. It was the story of the *Wild Soccer Bunch* against the

Furies, the story of the upset of the century.

My friends, let me tell you, I couldn't wait for the ending. As soon as the story was over, I jumped up, raced to the phone and called the *Wild Soccer Bunch,* one by one.

"Let's all meet at Camelot. Right now!" I said. "My mom's got a plan."

Meeting at Camelot

"A plan?" Kevin spat. "Your mother is clueless."

"No, she's not! She's a real gunslinger," I protested. Bad move.

"A what?" Kevin burst out. My friends didn't get the gunslinger thing. You had to be there. Now they thought I was positively mental.

We were at Camelot. It's actually Julian's tree house but we call it Camelot. He built it himself in his backyard, three-floors tall. It was our meeting place. We'd gather here when the chips were down, and it was here we'd always figure out a way through things. But this time, things seemed downright impossible.

The *Wild Soccer Bunch* was history. And my mother explained why: we had given up. Simple as that. But my friends didn't get it. No, they just stared at me like zombies, as if I was demented. No one listened to me.

I sat in a corner in the downstairs room, our conference hall, watching my friends.

Kevin was pacing nervously. "Did you hear that? Diego's mom is really a gunslinger!" He shouted and hit the wall so hard his fist began to bleed. "Oww! That's why you called us here? You've got to be kidding!"

No one dared say a word.

Danny tapped his feet and Tyler drummed his fingers on the table. Julian hugged his knees as if he was freezing, Josh chewed his fingernails, and Alex bit his lips. Joey pinched his arm, Kyle played with a golf ball, and Roger put curlers in his hair.

They looked like a bunch of total losers.

But at least they were here. I could see they were desperate. I had to do something, even if they laughed me out of town. I just had to, even though it was my mother's plan and they'd never get the gunslinger thing.

I took a deep breath and cleared my throat. "Ahem! Here goes. The plan is really quite simple. We play the *Furies*."

I paused to let it sink in. My friends rolled their eyes. And Kevin said it like it was.

"That's it?" he mocked. "Dude, we *know* that plan."

"Yes, we do," Danny agreed. "And it's absurd. The *Furies* will destroy us, then make us the laughing stock of every other team in town. And you know why? I'll tell you why. To them, we are nothing but pathetic little ants, trying to climb Mount Everest. They're on top, and they can't see us way down at the bottom because we're ants. In other words, we are nothing to them. Less than nothing. As far as they're concerned, we don't exist."

"Well, I guess we'll just have to change that." I said it calmly because I *was* calm.

"Yeah, right, and how exactly do you plan to do that?" Danny's eyes glistened with rage. "Tie a trunk to our noses and call us elephants?"

I pointed at Danny. "Good idea. You're close," I praised him.

They didn't buy it.

"Really," Danny spat. "All right. Let's hear this genius plan."

"Yeah, spit it out, Diego," Kevin added. "We can't *wait* to hear what you've got up your sleeve."

"Okay," I said accepting the challenge. "First of all, knock off the whining."

Everything went pin-drop quiet. All you could hear was the air whispering my friends' fury. Kevin and Danny clenched their fists and I was sure one false move would set them off.

"Excuse me?" Kevin hissed, insulted, but I just shook my head.

"I'm talking about all of us, including me," I said. "Actually, I was the worst whiner of us all. First I was petrified Joey and Kyle would kick me off the team. Then I was scared of Fabio. And then, until last night, I was hiding from the world, because I was so scared of the *Furies*. I was afraid I wasn't good enough. I was hoping we'd never play soccer again. My mom says be careful what you wish for because that's what you'll get, and guess what – we sure got it."

I looked around at my team. The hatred was gone. Even Kevin and Danny hung their heads low.

"I feel just like you," I continued. "I felt like I just

got run over by a truck. We can't let this happen. Nobody gets to treat us like dirt. Got that? And that's why we're here."

The others looked at me. It wasn't a pretty sight. Their eyes were blank. Now I was furious.

"I can't believe you guys! What's wrong with you? We're friends. And the *Wild Soccer Bunch* is the best soccer team in the world. Who cares if Ribaldo laughs at us? He bites!"

"Yeah, we'll show him!" Kevin and Danny shouted finally, and the others chimed in.

I was relieved. They finally woke up. They finally understood what was at stake. But I wasn't quite done yet.

"Hold it! One more thing. There's a catch."

I didn't continue until the excitement ebbed. "The *Furies* are one of the best youth soccer teams in the country. The very best kids play for them, and we can't expect them to take us seriously. Danny is right. As far as the *Furies* are concerned we're just a bunch of ants. We're the ants and they're the elephants, but guess what elephants hate the most? When ants crawl up their trunks. And that is exactly what we are going to do.

"Crawl up their trunks?" Danny asked.

"Yes," I answered. "So to speak. Which is why we need a plan."

"Duh! Haven't we already been through this?" Kevin asked and Danny smirked. "Spit it out already."

"Just so you know, it's my mother's plan," I warned them.

"And she's a gunslinger!" Josh threw in. The sparkle in his eyes was contagious.

I smiled proudly. Then I told them everything my mother had told me: we had to become like the *Furies* to become a real team. A real team needed a name and a club and a Charter; every player needed a contract; and on top of that, we needed jerseys with our own logo on it. And to get jerseys and soccer gear we needed someone who'd pay for them. We needed a sponsor.

If we had all that, we wouldn't be just a bunch of ball-kicking little kids with supersize dreams, attracting Giacomo Ribaldo's ridicule and Fabio's contempt. No, we'd be a team even the *Furies* would have to take seriously.

"What's the verdict?" I finished. "You think we can do it?"

"Of course we can!" Kevin answered.

"Yes, but where are we going to practice?" Tyler threw in. "What about Larry? You forgot about Larry, Diego."

"No, I didn't!" I answered. "I think this is exactly

what Larry wants us to do. Get back on the warpath."

Tyler's face burst into a huge smile and Kevin whistled.

"You got that right," he said and high-fived me.

"All's well that ends well," he smiled.

"No," I grinned, "all's well as long as you're *wild*."

The others joined in. From that moment on, that would be our slogan. The slogan that marked the *Wild Soccer Bunch*.

Never Give Up!

We were busy the next few days. First, we needed a name. That was a no-brainer. We were the *Wild Soccer Bunch*. Both Kevin and Tyler were into the European teams who would always add a couple of letters to the ends of their names, like F.C. They thought it would be great if we had some letters at the end of our name too. "They call it an acronym," he said, and we all agreed. But what?

Tyler nailed it immediately: "a.u."

"A.U.?" Kevin asked.

"No caps," Tyler grinned. "The *Wild Soccer Bunch a.u.*"

"I heard you, I have ears!" Kevin spat. "I'm asking you, what does 'a.u.' mean?"

"Don't you get it?" Tyler grinned. He loved teasing his brother, especially when he was boneheaded about something.

"It means, 'always united!'"

Kevin whistled. "The *Wild Soccer Bunch* always united I have to admit, that is *tight!*"

But then he furrowed his brow.

"You don't think it's too much? I mean, if we won't be together one day...?"

"Heck we will!!" Tyler said. "And anyway, nobody but us is going to know what it means. Even *you* didn't get it."

He smiled at Kevin, who really wanted to smack that demeaning grin off his face, but Tyler continued unfazed.

"Listen. The *a.u.* will be our secret code to each other. It will give us power. Make sense?"

"You are too much!" Kevin grinned, and so we all shook hands and agreed: we were officially the *Wild Soccer Bunch a.u.*

Armed with a drawing pad and colored pencils, Tyler went off by himself to design our jersey, our logo, and our player contracts; he disappeared into the Camelot tower, which was really the upper floor of the tree house. We didn't see or hear a peep out of him for two whole days, and he probably would have starved up there if it hadn't been for Julian's mother, who threw him some snacks and a drink every once in a while.

Joey, Kyle, Danny, Alex, Josh, Julian, and Roger took off to find a sponsor. Divide and conquer was their motto, and so they paid a visit to every car lot and sporting goods store in the area, splitting into groups of two to cover more ground. They went off proudly, heads held high, eyes on their goal and hearts sure of their success. They argued over how many sponsors they'd find, and whether it was okay to advertise on one's underwear.

Kevin and I remained in our meeting room, preparing the Charter. We wracked our brains for two whole days until we finally nailed it.

On the third day, we all reconvened in Camelot. We locked all the doors and windows and lit candles. Tyler stood in the center to show us his designs. His drawing was small, but fantastic. The jerseys were the one and only acceptable color: black as the night. The cleats were bright orange and the logo was a wild looking guy, simple and understated, like us. We were stoked. And we were even more excited about the player contracts. They looked like treasure maps, dark and mysterious. Naturally we signed them in fake blood. That was only fitting. Roger still had some left over from last Halloween. We even pretended it hurt, just to make it more real. After all, this was serious business. But first, Kevin and I read the rules of the Charter:

Rule number 1: "Be wild!" And the reason for that was our slogan, which was set in stone in Rule number 2:

"All's well as long as you're wild!"

Rule 3: "Never give up!"

Rule 4: "One for all and all for one."

And the last rule, Rule number 5: "Whoever leaves the *Wild Soccer Bunch* is a traitor."

It got real quiet after that. It was so quiet we could hear our neighbor down the street arguing with himself. Our rules were tough but fair, and they shaped us into a tight group where everyone mattered. We knew we could rely on each other unconditionally. There is nothing more important for a team. And with our jerseys, the

contracts, and our Charter, we were more than just
a team. We were a band of brothers, like the Three
Musketeers or Robin Hood's men. With one difference:
we wouldn't be fighting with swords or bows and arrows.
We'd be fighting with a ball on the soccer field.

Slowly and silently we all rose together. And then
solemnly, we all signed the contract. Then we formed a
circle, held each other by the shoulder and swore that
everything we had decided upon on this day would hold
forever. And we swore to it with an earth shattering
"1-2-3 wild!"

We only had to deal with one more minor detail. We
had to choose the sponsor who'd pay for our jerseys.
We looked to the seven who had gone out looking for
sponsors. But they remained somber.

"No sponsors," they said, finally spitting it out. They
were embarrassed and couldn't look us in the eye. They
said they had tried everything. They had been to every
single car lot and sporting goods store from Bushnell
to Michigan Avenue. They had visited gas stations,
laundromats, and coffee shops. Everywhere they went no
one took them seriously. Some were polite and friendly,
but some were downright mean. The worst guy was
this fast food drive-thru owner who looked like he ate
most of the junk he sold; an evil blubbery guy twice

the size of Mickey the bulldozer with a voice like a bear with a sore throat. "I'm never going to be Mr. America and you're never going to be real soccer players." He laughed and laughed and food flew out of his mouth and they got out of there as fast as their legs would take them.

Kevin, Tyler, and I couldn't believe it. We had been so close, and now this. Then Roger started squirming in his seat and shot his hand in the air, waving it wildly, wanting us to call on him like we were in school.

"I may know a sponsor," he blurted out, and everyone hung on his next words.

"My uncle is a butcher," Roger continued, "and I'm sure he'd happily support us if we put his logo on our shirts. If we did that, he'd even give us all the hot dogs we could eat, every time we played."

Roger then proudly pulled out a drawing of his uncle's logo. It was a hot dog on two legs with a pig face.

Silence.

"You've got to be kidding," Kevin hissed at him, but Roger remained firm.

"We could uh... sell the hot dogs," he said seriously.

"Sure we could." Kevin couldn't believe it. "And we could call ourselves the *Wild Soccer Wienies*."

It took him a while, but Roger finally got the picture.

He saw the horror in our faces and lowered his head, mortified. "Okay, so maybe we just don't get any jerseys."

That wouldn't work either, but Roger was right. My mother's plan had failed. We'd never be a real team without jerseys.

"Whoa, wait a second, we can't bail now," Danny protested. "We just violated Rule number 1: 'Never give up!' We all swore to that."

Danny was right, too. Like I told you, he always knows what to do. He always finds a way out. The word 'impossible' is not in his vocabulary. Luckily for us, he had a plan this time, too. "I know this guy," he said. "We'll go pay him a visit tomorrow. All we have to do is bring our piggy banks. And put some gel in our hair and wear our shades. That should do it."

We had no idea what he was talking about. But it was Danny, so it didn't matter. With Danny, we had blind faith.

An Offer You Can't Refuse

The next day after school we followed Danny into town.
We all put gel in our hair and wore black sunglasses –
we were looking real cool. Under our arms we carried our
piggy banks, tin cans, pillow cases, hollowed-out stuffed
animals or whatever we used to stash our allowance. We
still had no idea what Danny was planning, not until we
stood right in front of the bank. Alex's father's bank. It
was as fancy as his house on Woodlawn Avenue.

Alex didn't even stop. He turned around on the spot
and backtracked the way we came. He had no intention
of dealing with his father's bank. To be honest, none of
us did.

We were thinking about being grounded for life,
the kind of punishment banks dish out for breaking
windows. We all wanted to leave with Alex, but that
didn't work. Escape was impossible. Alex didn't get far
either.

"Stop, Alex. Not another step!" Danny's voice boomed
and made Alex stop dead in his tracks.

"We all swore to uphold our Charter. So rules number three, four and five are now in effect. You didn't forget them already, did you?"

Alex shook his head. He looked desperate as he inched his way further and further from us. Danny watched him for a few endless heartbeats. Then he said loudly, but calmly: "Rule number three: Never give up! Rule number 4: One for all and all for one. Rule number 5: Whoever leaves the *Wild Soccer Bunch*... is a traitor."

Alex took two more steps. Then he stopped and turned around, stared us down for a moment, then came back to the rest of us with his head hung low. Danny smiled. He waited until Alex stood right in front of him. Then he put his arm around his shoulder: "Alex, my man, it won't be that bad. I promise, we're not going to rob your dad's bank." He grinned. "We're going to make him an offer he can't refuse."

Then he turned to us.

"Okay, and the rest of you, you're going to do what you always do when you are as scared out of your mind as I am. You're going to look cool. And leave the rest to me. Trust me, I know what I'm doing. My dad told me this story. How *The Rolling Stones* – one of the most famous rock bands in the world – got the best record deal in history."

We had no idea what he was talking about. Most of us never even heard of *The Rolling Stones*. And that was the beauty of the plan. We didn't need to know. We just needed to look cool.

Danny opened the door to the bank and started whistling again the song his father would always whistle whenever he was scared: 'Knock, Knock, Knocking on Heaven's Door.'

We were scared, all right, but we had no choice... we needed our jerseys.

When we marched in, the bank clerks looked at us as if we were demented. I could totally understand. Roger stood next to me; his hair slicked back, shades low on his nose, a polka-dotted pillowcase full of allowance under his arm. I'm sure they never saw anyone like us before.

The bank fell quiet in an instant and the only sound that broke the silence was Danny, whistling his tune. He looked from one clerk to the next, furrowed his brow, scratched his ear and finally let the whistle die down.

Now it was really quiet and mortifying. But mortifying situations are Danny's specialty. This was no exception, and as always, Danny dug out his irresistible smile.

"Good afternoon, ladies and gentlemen," he said with polite resolve. "You may not believe this, but we'd like to see the manager."

One of the clerks choked trying to hide his sense of alarm. He coughed and gagged and finally spat up an answer: "I'm sorry, but the manager is a very busy man."

"Aren't we all," Danny answered with confidence. "Why wouldn't he be? He's under a lot of pressure. Fortunately for all of us, we have an appointment."

"Oh really!" the clerk mocked us, looked at his colleagues and rolled his eyes. "An appointment with the manager?"

"Precisely," Danny responded, unfazed by the mockery. "I'm glad you're able to keep up."

The clerk gagged again, gasped for air, and wanted to say something, but Danny cut him off. "Would you please be so kind and announce our presence?" Danny grinned. "Just tell the manager that the gentlemen from the *W.S.B. a.u.* have arrived."

The clerk was flabbergasted, but Danny's determined smile didn't allow any objections. The clerk obeyed and staggered into the manager's office. And because the manager was also Alex's dad, we were terrified.

"Have you completely lost your mind?" I whispered. "What are you talking about, we don't have an appointment!"

"Incorrect, Diego, my man," Danny smiled. "I called Alex's dad yesterday explaining that our company wanted to settle right here in this fair city."

"I see. And which company would that be?" I asked.

"Why, the *Wild Soccer Bunch,* of course," Danny answered. "I just used a slightly abbreviated version of our name – *W.S.B. a.u.* Kapiche?"

"And he bought it?"

"Yes. Well, I disguised my voice, of course. Like this ..." Danny dropped his voice an octave. "You know, Mr. Alexander, there are several banks we are looking at, but..."

"But...?" I interrupted impatiently.

"Long story short, he cancelled three appointments to meet with us. I'm telling you, he can't wait to meet us. Check him out!" Danny grinned.

Alex's father stormed from his office, his back still turned towards us while he read his employee the riot act.

"I don't care for your behavior one bit, Mr. Weber. Your attitude is detrimental to our business. Of course I'll meet with the gentlemen from the *W.S.B. a.u.*"

With that, he spun on his heel with a big grin plastered across his face. And then he saw us, and froze in place, his jaw slack.

"Weber!" he yelled. "What is happening here?"

We froze, too, and wanted nothing more than to blend into the marble floor. Josh fussed with his stuffed animal and Roger chewed on his pillowcase. But Danny was unfazed. He was one cool dude.

"Good afternoon, Mr. Alexander!" he said with a voice too deep for his size, grinned, and then spoke in his normal boy's voice. "It's very generous of you, indeed, to spare a moment of your precious time. Come on, guys," he said, and then he marched right into the manager's office.

We followed him with buckling knees. Alex's father was the last to slip into his office, closing the door behind him.

"What is the meaning of this?" he hissed. "Do you realize who I am? I can't imagine what my employees are thinking of me right now!"

We flinched, but Danny stayed cool.

"Why Mr. Alexander, that's exactly why we're here," he smiled. "But first I have to explain a few things. Why don't you take a seat? All we need is ten minutes of your time. I promise we'll have an agreement by then."

Alex's father gasped for air. I cringed, expecting him to spit fire and burn us to a crisp, but instead of blowing us away, Alex's father was hypnotized by

Danny's irresistible smile and did as he was told, sat right down behind his desk.

"All right. Ten minutes. Not a second more." Danny didn't waste any time. He told him the whole story, about Fabio, Ribaldo, and Larry, who had doomed us to hell, and the game we had to play against the *Furies*. He told him about our soccer club, the contracts and the Charter, and the urgent need for our own jersey. He explained that jerseys were necessary for the *Furies* to take us seriously, but that we were caught in a serious dilemma. We needed sponsors to buy us the soccer gear, but the sponsors needed us to win a big victory before they could justify plunking down their cold hard cash for our soccer gear. That, Danny explained, was why we were there, at the bank, and in his office.

Danny paused dramatically and Alex's father leaned back behind his huge desk. For a second, we thought Danny had impressed him. But instead, Alex's father looked at his watch and said: "That was eight minutes. You have two left."

Danny took a deep breath. Then he said simply: "OK. You're right. Let's get down to business. I have three estimates for the soccer gear. One seems reasonable. $800. We have $400. Guys, piggy banks on the table." We all slapped our banks on the table and the office sounded like a line of slot machines going off.

"You will fund the rest, and by you, I mean your bank, but only until we play the game. For the game, we invite all potential sponsors, especially those who didn't believe in us. After our victory, they will be stepping all over themselves to cover out debts."

Danny paused again and waited for the adulation, but Alex's father only looked at the mountain of piggy banks, tin cans, cigar boxes, hollowed out stuffed animals and pillowcases on his desk.

"And what if you lose?" he asked coldly.

"Well, there is... that risk," Danny smiled politely. "There's never a deal without a risk." We all smiled and nodded dumbly.

Alex's father smiled, too.

"You have one more minute. But I might as well tell you right now: that's no risk, it's a death sentence."

Danny nodded, and thought for a moment.

"I see, I understand," he said. "I really do."

But then he sighed deeply.

"But we have to come to an agreement anyway. You know, we don't want to be cruel or anything, but we really have no choice. We need the soccer gear . And so, it is my duty to remind you of your employees. I can imagine they're out there making fun of you right now, as we speak, because you've been negotiating with us for quite a long time. What would they say if they knew your son broke two living room windows and you never punished him, and all because your daughter was dancing like an insane cheerleader? Do you really believe that would nurture your managerial authority?"

There it was, the offer Danny had talked about, the offer Alex's father couldn't refuse. Mr. Alexander leaned back in his chair, cool as a cucumber, but the sweat on his upper lip betrayed his bluff.

"You'd do that?" he asked, looking at us one by one. "You'd really do that?" he asked again, this time looking at Alex, his own son.

Alex didn't say a word. None of us did. We listened to Danny and finally understood the genius of his plan. The slicked back hair and the shades made us look merciless, and that's why Alex's dad took the offer.

"Fine," he sighed. "You win. But if you lose to the *Furies* and don't find a sponsor, I will personally confiscate those jerseys, you got that?"

We nodded, and then we left the bank calmly, but as quickly as possible. Mission accomplished. Now we had a chance to win against the *Furies*. But no, there was one more thing we needed: our coach, Larry! Would he come back and coach us? Or would he send us packing, because he still didn't believe in us?

We all knew, if Larry didn't believe in us, we could forget the soccer gear. We'd never play soccer again. We'd release ourselves from the solemn oath we had sworn with each other, and go study underwater basket weaving. That was about the size of it. And it scared us.

None of us wanted to do any of that, and so, with great humility and hunger because it was way past our lunchtime, we ran straight from the bank to the soccer field to find Larry.

All Eggs in One Basket

"So, what do you say, are you with us?" Kevin asked, as cool as a cucumber, as if it didn't really matter at all.

Larry sat in his rocking chair, calmly looking at what we had brought along: the jersey designs, the Charter and the player contracts.

"Come on, Larry, make up your mind already. We don't have all day!" Kevin demanded, and even I didn't think he was bluffing.

Larry didn't think so either. He looked at us, and luckily we were still wearing our shades, or Larry would have seen that our eyes were begging him to join us. He pushed his cap back onto his neck thoughtfully, and scratched his forehead.

"Man! You're sure singing a different tune now," he mumbled. Then he threw another glance at the rules and contracts.

"This is serious stuff, I think. Like you're putting all your eggs in one basket."

He scratched his forehead one more time.

"If you lose to the *Furies*, your allowance will be gone for the next two years, maybe even longer."

He eyeballed us again, but we hid behind our shades and remained silent.

"I don't know," Larry thought out loud, "but I guess this is the way it's got to be. It's something about those sunglasses." Then he snapped his fingers as if he suddenly realized the truth. "I got it! Your sunglasses are like your war paint, your very own, very cool war paint. Am I right?"

We burst out in smiles all around. Even Kevin couldn't

keep from smiling, he was that relieved. But Larry remained serious.

"Too bad, though," he sighed. "Really too bad I can't be your coach."

That wiped the smile right off our faces. Our knees buckled and we staggered back a few steps. But Larry wasn't done yet.

"I mean you've got to understand. These are players' contracts. I don't see a coach's contract. I can't work like this. Coaches are always on the hot seat these days. If something bad happens — I take the heat. I can't coach the *Wild Soccer Bunch* without a contract."

Did Larry just say what I thought he said? An avalanche of rocks fell off my chest, as Tyler rummaged through his backpack.

"Larry, I'm glad you brought that up," he said, beaming. "I just happen to have a coaching contract right here!"

He handed it to Larry, who opened it immediately and read it out loud.

"Contract for the best coach in the world. The small print is our Charter. Therefore the contract cannot be terminated, unless you are a traitor or no longer wild and voluntarily join a basket weaving class."

Larry thought long and hard and scratched his

forehead again.

"Wow! This is really serious. I don't know," he murmured and handed the contract back to Tyler. "I left my fake blood at home," he grumbled looking right at us. Kevin grinned and pulled a bottle out of his pocket and showed it to him.

Larry just smiled. "Looks like you boys thought of everything," he said and sealed the deal, pressing his thumbprint on the contract and swearing our oath.

"All's well," he began, and we all finished along with him "...as long as you're wild!"

Then we wrote a polite letter to the *Furies*. It was our sincere wish to play them in three weeks from Sunday. We suggested that specific date because that's how long it would take for our jerseys to get here, and three weeks would be enough time for us to get ready. At least that's what we thought, fueled by our newfound courage and confidence. Lucky for us, we had no idea how good a team the *Furies* really were.

The Challenge

We took the letter to school the next day. Fabio himself would have to be the one to bring it to the *Furies*. We really didn't have to discuss this. It was a question of honor and pride. Fabio and his arrogant father would be the first to find out that the *Wild Soccer Bunch a.u.* never gives up.

"All's well!" We welcomed each other as we arrived at school one by one. "As long as you're wild!" We all gathered at the stairwell that led from the yard to the school building and sat down on the steps. The first bell rang and the other kids stormed past us into their classrooms. In no time the yard was a ghost town. The weather was still wild. It was June, but it was chilly and grey like November. The wind howled, blowing dust out into the street like a thick fog. We could hardly make out the entrance to the playground, and that's why Fabio didn't see us when he finally arrived.

Like every day, he showed up at the last minute. We knew why. Since we had paid him a visit at Heaven's

Gate 9, he avoided us and we ignored him. That's why the last thing Fabio expected that day was to see us waiting for him when he arrived.

He walked toward us, staring at his feet. For a moment I didn't recognize him. He didn't look anything like the beaming boy on the first day of school. Maybe it was just the gloomy weather, but I could have sworn he looked sad, lonely and worst of all... unhappy. For a brief moment I forgot what he had done to us and that he was the enemy. In that moment, I was sure he missed us, especially when he saw us. A smile flittered across his face like a ray of sunshine. But when he realized we wanted something, his smile disappeared, and loneliness and sadness were replaced with icy pride. Yes, Fabio was as wild as any one of us. He would have been a perfect addition to our team. But that was no longer possible. He was our opponent and our enemy. Proudly, he held his head up high and marched directly towards us.

Kevin gave the sign and we all stood up together. Fabio didn't flinch. We stood in his way like a dark threatening wall. For a moment all you could hear was the howling wind. Then Kevin stepped towards him. The two of them were so close their noses almost touched.

"Hello, Kevin," Fabio said calmly, but Kevin had no

time for formalities.

"Do you have any idea why we're here?" he asked Fabio coldly, the way you talk to your opponent during a game.

"I can guess," Fabio said, never even blinking.

"Good!" Kevin responded. "Then please take this letter to the *Furies*."

He pushed the letter into Fabio's chest. Fabio took it and looked at it. The envelope was black and sealed with our logo. Again a smile flittered over Fabio's face. Was it joy, as I thought, or mockery? Kevin must have thought it was mockery.

"One more thing. Tell your father, and anyone else who thinks we're not worthy – we're not going to take it anymore."

Kevin riveted him with hostility, but remained calm. He stepped aside to let Fabio pass. But then Fabio did something I didn't expect him to do: he hesitated. He looked at us, one by one. Finally his eyes met mine; it was as if he looked directly into my heart and at that moment I almost felt sorry for him. But then, without a word, he was gone, walking up the stairs and disappearing into the building. Kevin looked after him and pumped his fist.

"Yeah!" he shouted, raising his hand for a high five:

"All's well!"

"As long as you're wild!" Danny answered, slapping Kevin's hand.

Then we followed Fabio into our classroom.

Grass Is Red

The next two weeks went by in a flash. We practiced every day and along with our newfound enthusiasm, summer returned as well. Larry really coached us hard, but unlike the practices we had for the game against the *Unbeatables* in the fly-infested park by the lake, nobody complained. This time we were ready to give it our all. Without protest we repeated every single exercise until Larry was satisfied. We'd play one-on-one for hours, fighting over the ball as if our lives depended on it. We'd drive shoulder against shoulder, slide into the ball at the last minute, but wouldn't stay down long; instead we'd get up immediately and keep fighting for the ball. We'd stop the ball no matter how high or how low it was, and we'd stop it with whatever body part it

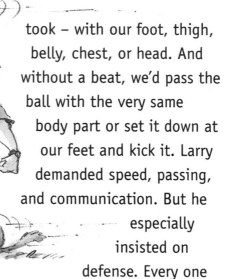

took – with our foot, thigh, belly, chest, or head. And without a beat, we'd pass the ball with the very same body part or set it down at our feet and kick it. Larry demanded speed, passing, and communication. But he especially insisted on defense. Every one of us had to be everywhere. Yes, even Kevin, our star striker, had to play defense during the counterattack. We ran and ran and ran, until we were ready to drop. And then we ran some more. We ran and ran until our legs buckled, but never our resolve.

I'm not kidding. Our legs would collapse in the middle of a sprint or a jump or a shot and we'd fall onto the grass as if slain by a sword. I'm talking utter exhaustion. We were lying in the grass dead as a doornail, absolutely sure we'd never ever get up again. But then Larry came to the rescue with ice-cold lemonade for us all, watched us wet our lips, and waited calmly for us to catch our breaths. Then he'd build us up again.

"That's all you've got?" he asked dryly. We looked up at him innocently, but remained silent. Larry eyeballed us again. "If that's how it is going to be you might as well *forget* the game against the *Furies*. You got that? The *Furies* is a top-rated youth club. They have kids who will end up in Major League Soccer in a few years. It's a different ball game altogether. You'll see. Soon as the whistle blows, the grass changes color. Green is red. They don't just have one brick-wall center defender like Julian Fort Knox. They have seven of him. You're going to feel like you are all alone with 28 men against you. So, what are you waiting for? Get up."

We stayed down. We couldn't get up, because at that moment all we thought was, what's the point? That's when Larry came up to me – to me, not to Kevin or to Danny. He knelt down in front of me. "What's up with your asthma, Diego? I mean, usually, when I work you

111

out too hard, you rattle like an elephant seal."

The question caught me by surprise, so I took a careful breath. I expected the usual rattle and the pain in my lungs, but there was nothing. That's when I realized that since the applesauce duel with my mom the gunslinger, I had not had a single attack. I looked at Larry.

"I guess that's because you're not asking too much!" I smiled and so did Larry.

"That's right, and you're getting better and better. In fact, I'm proud of all of you!"

I got up. I had to be first to get up because I was always the first to go down. I had to get up to hide my emotions from Larry and my friends. And I had another reason, too: I wasn't tired any more.

"Hey guys, Larry is right! We're not only getting in better shape every day, we're becoming better soccer players!" I shouted. My energy was contagious. With that, we continued practicing long into the evening, and then floated home as if on clouds.

You know the feeling when your body is completely exhausted and you still feel light as a feather? It was a great feeling. We all walked home together, and as we parted, one after another, we solemnly said:

"All's well!" And the others responded just as solemnly: "As long as you're wild!"

The Helpful Penguin

On day 15 after the challenge, we arrived at school. This time Fabio was waiting for *us*. Like we waited for him two weeks earlier, he sat on the steps that led from the playground to the building. But he didn't get up when we approached. He stayed put, took the letter from his pocket and handed it to us without a word. He looked at us and I wondered how anybody could be so unhappy. But maybe, I thought, maybe he's only playing it cool and just being plain arrogant. Yes, that seemed to suit him much better.

Whatever. We didn't dare open Fabio's letter right away. But inside, we were exploding with anticipation. It was too late to do anything about it because school was about to start, so we all agreed to wait until school was out, that way we could open it in front of the greatest coach in the world, Larry.

On the field, Larry took out his pocket knife and opened the envelope. Then he unfolded the piece of paper carefully, and quietly read it twice, pushed his cap back and scratched his forehead. Then he read the letter out loud:

"Dear *Wild Soccer Bunch!*" he read, and we sighed, moaned in pain, and rolled our eyes. What kind of greeting was that? 'Dear' and 'wild' didn't exactly go together.

"Dear *Wild Soccer Bunch!*" Larry repeated, and he had a hard time hiding his irritation. "Dear *Wild Soccer Bunch!* Thank you very much for your 'challenge.' 'Challenge' is in quotes," Larry spat it out with disdain. "Unfortunately, the *Furies* Youth Club is fully booked. With kind regards, the Club Administrator."

Larry scanned us, eyeing each and every one of us. "That's not all," he said. "There's an addition. 'P.S.: Dear *Wild Soccer Bunch,* please understand that the *Furies* prefer to play opponents who are on the same level, and therefore cannot respond to further inquiries'."

It was quiet. So quiet you could hear, taste, and smell our own anger. Our fury gathered like a thunderstorm on the horizon, and then it erupted like a volcano...

"That's an insult!" Tyler yelled.

"Arrogant morons!" Kevin cursed.

"They can kiss my goal post!" Danny shouted. And I added furiously: "They didn't take us seriously. They won't even *consider* playing us."

Sheesh. That shut us up but good.

Our ferocity leaked from us like hot air from a punctured balloon.

There was no way to answer this kind of an insult. It was like the weather forecast. Rain tomorrow. Period. The end. Nothing you could do. We were powerless. Kevin kicked the grass angrily.

"Stupid jerks!" he shouted. "You know what? They don't deserve to play us!"

He looked at us, thinking it would cheer us up, but it didn't. Without a word, disappointed and humiliated yet again, we sat down in the grass and picked at it as if we were a bunch of depressed sheep. Even Larry sat down. And it didn't help that he pushed his cap back and scratched his forehead. Obviously he didn't know what to do either.

Then Kyle broke the silence.

"Kevin is right. They don't deserve us. And I think that's exactly how we'll get to them. Come on!"

Kyle jumped up.

"Come on, let's go. There's not much time. It's already one thirty and we have to talk to Edgar before my mom crawls out of the salad bowl."

We had no idea what he was talking about, but Kyle was already gone and we had no choice but to follow him.

"You know," he explained as we were running along. "My mother is an actress. That's why she always wears cucumbers on her eyes and yogurt on her face. Every day until two in the afternoon. That's when the paparazzi and the gossip columnists show up..."

"What are they doing? asked Josh.

"My mom is famous so everyone wants to catch a glimpse of her and hear what she has to say." Kyle said. "And Edgar is in charge of the whole thing. It's called publicity."

"Well, publicize this," Josh said and punched the doorbell.

A moment later, Edgar the penguin opened the door. By penguin, I mean Edgar, the butler, of course. It's the black tuxedo and tails he wears when he's working. He looks like a penguin. That day, his face was carved in wood and his nose hung in the clouds like the Goodyear Blimp. He did that to tell those who had no business there, that they had no business *being* there. But he treated us differently. With us, his wooden face softened and turned into a wide friendly waxy grin.

"Hi Edgar, which paper is coming out here today?" Kyle cut to the chase and didn't waste any time. But Edgar morphed back into wood, put his nose up in the clouds, and insisted on the procedure he always required whenever he saw us.

"Nononono. Not like zat, messieurs. First, ze code."

What code?

"Right!" Kyle realized. "All's well!"

"Az long az you are wild! Exactement," Edgar smiled again. "And now, messieurs. Vat can I do for you?"

"C'mon, Edgar, I already told you," Kyle grumbled. "Which journalist is coming today? We need an interview."

"We need publicity!" Josh agreed.

"With pictures! Please tell us which paper is it today, Edgar?"

"Ze guys from Ze *Daily Paper,* but oh mon dieu, zey are zo terribly ordinary."

"That's perfect, Edgar," Kyle shouted excitedly. "That's exactly what we need. Can you talk them into writing about us in exchange for a big story on mom tomorrow?"

Kyle looked at Edgar with his big, round E.T.-looking eyes. And suddenly the penguin was no longer made of wax, but of ice, melting in the sun.

"Olala, monsieur. Zat von't be cheap. Zat will cost dearly. Zat will cost you... an honorary membership in ze *Wild Soccer Bunch*." He grinned broadly.

We all laughed. That was a done deal. Ten minutes later we sat in the garage, had our picture taken, and talked to the journalist and the photographer. At first they behaved like the *Furies*. In other words, arrogant. But we wore them down and finally got to them. Half an hour into the interview, they were on our side, and when we went to thank them, they just smiled.

"All's well" they said. "As long as you're wild!" We responded with a grin. And it was with that same grin that Larry showed us the paper the next day when we dropped by his stand before school. Hot off the presses, our picture still glistening in ink. But the picture wasn't all. Above it, in big fat black letters, the headline announced:

"THE *FURIES* AREN'T WILD ENOUGH FOR THE *WILD SOCCER BUNCH*"

Sweet! This is going to slap them right in the face. Even the *Furies* won't be able to handle this kind of an insult. And sure as the sun comes up every morning, two days later, Fabio brought a second letter to school, and it read simply: "We accept your challenge. Sunday, 9:30 a.m. Our practice field."

At that moment, we were unstoppable. We called all the potential sponsors who had turned us down and invited them to the game. We even asked the fast-food drive-thru owner. Yeah, we were smug. It was gratifying, I tell you. Our supply of energy seemed endless, and so we practiced even harder. Everything worked, no matter what we did, and the word 'exhaustion' wasn't in our vocabulary. Only school and our bed times interrupted our practice; the nights got shorter and shorter. When it was too dark to see, Alex pulled out his most prized possession: an orange glow-in-the-dark soccer ball. With that we'd play until our parents showed up at the soccer field to take us home.

On the Friday before the game, as the sun disappeared behind the trees, our hard work finally paid off. Larry called us all over to his stand as he dug out a big box and put it down in front of us. He called us up, one by one, reached into the box and handed us a package wrapped in white. It felt like an awards ceremony, like we were being knighted. When he finally let us open our packages, we were breathless, drained, and tongue-tied for the first time in a week. Our jerseys were black as night with a bright orange logo and bright orange cleats – they felt like gold in our hands.

Larry smiled, scratching his forehead to hide his emotions.

"What are you waiting for? They aren't tablecloths," he said hoarsely. "Put them on already!" He didn't have to tell us twice. It took all of ten seconds and we were ready for action. We looked at each other happily, gently touched the orange cleats on our feet and felt the texture of the orange logo on our chests.

Dude! We had waited a long time for this moment. Larry took out his camera and snapped a picture of us. No need for the flash, we were glowing with pride.

Then, all of a sudden, Larry got real serious. He knelt down in the grass before us and looked at us for a long time.

He finally said: "I'm proud of you. You're a real team and I hope you will stay a team forever. Even if you don't win on Sunday."

Say what? We were stunned. Why would he say something like that? Did he want to crush our hopes? Didn't he realize what was at stake? Defeat was out of the question. We'd lose everything. We'd be ruined for years and Alex's dad would confiscate the jerseys. But Larry dismissed our protests.

"Listen, you need to think about this. What I'm about to tell you is as important as practice. Believe me, some time tonight, fear will creep up on you. The fear that, despite everything we've done, you might lose. If this fear is still in your bones when you play the *Furies* on Sunday, you'll never win. And if it is fear that makes you lose, it's all over. Everything will have been in vain... and the *Wild Soccer Bunch* will be no more."

We were dumbstruck, but Larry wiped his sweaty palms on his pants and stood up.

"Time to go, guys. Time to go home. No practice tomorrow. See you Sunday at 9 sharp on the *Furies'* field. And make sure you get a good night's sleep on Saturday."

The Dare

We slinked home without a word. Larry was absolutely right. That night, which was Friday night, fear crept up on us. At first we didn't take it seriously. We thought it was Larry's fault. We thought he had somehow planted it into our minds and that it would be gone the next day. But it wasn't. The next day the fear was so bad we didn't even want to talk to each other. Tyler didn't even speak to Kevin, his own brother; instead, he read a book, something he hadn't done in ages. But truth be told, he didn't read. He just stared at the pages and the funny little black squiggles, never realizing he was holding the book upside-down.

At some point or another each one of us picked up the phone to call someone else on the team, but at the other end, all we got was ringing. Not one of us was ready to face his fear. All we could think of was: 'Larry's right. We're never going win this.'

I had been hiding in my room all day when my mother called me for dinner. She had made pancakes again and that gave me an idea: "Mom," I asked her, "could you be a gunslinger again?"

My mother looked at me with surprise. Then she shrugged her shoulders, grabbed the spoon, and said with a deep and husky voice. "Whattaya need, pardner? Didn't get enough of me last time?"

I shook my head.

"No, not like that, mom. We don't have to play this game again. I need to talk to you. I mean, really, you know... man to man."

For a moment it was all quiet. My mother gulped some air and mustered up some courage. After all, she was the best mom in the whole wide world. She understood, and I could tell her anything. I told her about the fear, and that we had to get rid of it or we'd never win, and as we were talking 'man to man', my mother came up with an idea.

"You need a dare," she said. "Remember the old wooden bridge above the pond in the park?? The one you wanted to jump off with your dad? You need to go there, and I mean right now."

"But... it's getting dark!" I protested. The bridge my mother was talking about was over 8 feet high. "We're supposed to go to bed early, Larry said. And besides, last year you got real mad at me, and I didn't even jump."

"Well, last year I was your mother," she smiled. "And I was glad you were chicken. But now we're talking man to man. And what do you think Larry would prefer? That you lose a little sleep or lose your lunch 'cause you're scared?"

I was shocked. I couldn't believe she was saying these things. Just thinking about the bridge made me dizzy. I could feel the fear run down my back like a trickle of cold water. What if we couldn't jump? That would take care of the game, once and for all. But my mom was the gunslinger, and as you know, gunslingers show no mercy. She reached under the table and grabbed a backpack.

"Go get a towel and your swim trunks and I'll make you a thermos of warm cider," she smiled. "Then go get the others. I'll meet you there."

I swallowed, but I had no choice. I took the backpack and filled it with my stuff, then grabbed my bike from the basement and took off. First I rode to Tyler and Kevin's house, and together we rode to Danny's, then to Julian and Josh's house. Then we picked up Roger and Alex and, with Josh's and Edgar's help, we finally smuggled Kyle past his father and out the door of the mansion.

"The gunslinger knows how we can face our fears," I just said, and the others nodded, grabbed their things, and followed me blindly. I didn't mention the bridge. I was afraid they wouldn't come if I did. In my mind, jumping from the old wooden bridge into the cold water of the pond was about as dangerous as climbing Mount Everest without oxygen. My only chance was to get them all there and hope that nobody would chicken out.

I stopped in the middle of the bridge and leaned my bike against the railing. I looked around for the gunslinger and saw her standing in the shadows down by the water where nobody else could see her. Then I turned towards the others. It was dark now, and the moon painted my friends' faces the colors of fear and trepidation. Pale and terrified, they held on to their bikes and glared at me.

"You're nuts!" Kevin was the first to realize what I was asking them to do.

"It's impossible!" Danny shouted.

"And as far as I'm concerned," Roger said decisively, "I wouldn't even think about it. I won't jump!"

"Fine. Suit yourselves," I said. "But I will. I'm sick of being afraid. I've been giving in to fear for far too long."

With that, I undressed and sat on top of the railing. Then I turned around one more time. My breath was hard and rattled.

"You know, I have asthma whenever I'm afraid. Like right now. But it's just my fear."

I stood up and looked down into the black abyss. The reflection of the moon and the clouds glistened on the surface of the water. I was thinking like Roger. I didn't want to jump. I saw myself disappear in the black water forever, sinking deeper and deeper.
My knees buckled. My heart raced.
Fear ran down my back.
But there was no
way out. "NO!" I
screamed – and
jumped. The others
threw their bikes
down, ran over
to the railing,
and saw me
disappear in the
black stream.
The impact was
hard and the water was cold. But then everything softened. I was light as a bird and floated back to the surface. And there, although I had to gasp for air, I wasn't afraid any more. My asthma – gone. I felt relieved and I was beaming with joy.

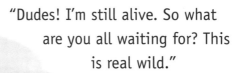

"Dudes! I'm still alive. So what are you all waiting for? This is real wild."

But the others looked at me as if they couldn't believe I had actually survived that jump. So I swam to shore, got out of the water and ran back up to the bridge.

"Okay, now we'll all jump in together. Come on, take off your clothes and let's do it, or you'll always believe you're a chicken. You too, Kevin." I looked directly into Kevin's eyes. "All for one and one for all."

Biting his lips, anger and fear in his eyes, he nodded. "Diego is right!"

A minute later, we all stood on the railing staring into the inky black abyss. I could feel their fear, I could almost taste it. Roger, who stood next to me, took my hand.

"All's well," I said.

"As long as you're wild," Roger and the others finished, softly but with determination.

Then we all jumped into the darkness, and each and every one of us let out a scream to ward off the fear. AAAAaaaahhhhh..!!

The water swallowed us whole and the world went black. But black was our team color, and once the fear was gone we were as light as a feather.

I caught a glimpse of the shore and the gunslinger. She tipped her hat in admiration to all of us.

We floated through the water like majestic sea lions, and as we cut through to the surface, we roared our joy all the way up to the stars.

Judgment Day

The next day started out calm and relaxed. It was Sunday, Judgment Day, but we were not the least bit anxious. We met Larry at the gate to the soccer field at 9 a.m. Although we didn't tell him anything about the dare on the bridge, he seemed to know what had happened. Our shining eyes gave it all away.

"Well done," he just said. Then he took his motorcycle and we followed him on our bikes.

We reached the practice grounds of the *Furies* on South Harlem Avenue. The field was huge, and because it was Sunday morning, it was still deserted. At first we didn't know where to turn, but then we caught sight of our opponents.

The U10 team of the *Furies* was waiting for us near the locker rooms. They sat on their bags quietly, looking us up and down. They didn't say a word, not even when we marched past them to the locker room. But their gazes said everything. The newspaper article had hurt their pride and honor, and they were determined to fix that. Only Fabio avoided our look, staring at his feet, obviously uncomfortable.

It was dead quiet in the locker room. All you could hear was the rustle of clothes as we put on our jerseys. We acted as if we had done this a million times. Then Larry called us all over to announce the line-up.

Kyle the invincible would be goalie, of course. Julian Fort Knox would play center fullback. Alex would play right fullback, and our number 10 Tyler, the man with the hardest kick in the world, would be his left fullback. Danny, the world's fastest midfielder, and Joey the magician, would play left and right wings. That left Kevin, our top striker at center forward.

Then Larry turned to Roger and me.

"Don't worry," he said. "Nobody will be left out today. You two will relieve Danny and Joey when they get tired."

"What about me?" Josh said, disappointed.

Larry looked at him surprised. Josh was three years younger than everybody else, and two heads smaller. He wouldn't have a chance against the *Furies*. But he was determined. Larry pushed his cap back far and scratched his forehead.

"You're my assistant," he said, but that didn't do it for Josh. And so Larry added: "And maybe you're our wild card, too."

"What's a wild card?" Josh asked.

"Something like a superhero," Larry smiled and Josh beamed.

Then Larry happily took the lead and marched us out onto the field.

Things had changed out there. The field was no longer deserted. All our parents had arrived. Even Joey's mother was there, and Edgar, the penguin. But that wasn't all. Kyle rubbed his eyes and tugged on my sleeve. His mother stood next to Edgar the butler and next to her stood his father, the man who despised soccer.

"It's great he's here," Kyle hissed. "But, if we lose, I'll *never* get out of being a golf pro."

Alex felt his father's gaze upon him. He was standing among the sponsors – the car dealers, the gas station owners and the computer specialists – watching his money. The money we had borrowed from his bank to pay for our gear.

But Kevin didn't care. He looked past all spectators and drilled his eyes into our real enemy, Giacomo Ribaldo, the Brazilian superstar, who was warming up on the adjacent field. When he felt Kevin's gaze upon him, he stayed cool and acted as if he was there by pure chance. Right.

Then we ran onto the field, past the fat fast food drive-thru owner, whose mocking gaze bounced off us like a tennis ball hitting a wall.

We were full of self-confidence. Everything had worked during warm-up. One of Kevin's bicycle kicks even made the *Furies* stop dead in their tracks to watch. At least, I'd like to think it was that, and not the referee's whistle that called us over to center field.

Greetings were icy. The *Furies* won kick-off. They were cool, calm, and collected. And just like that, Fabio took the ball and jogged from midfield towards our goal. Then, as sudden and fast as lightning, he passed the ball. The *Furies'* midfielder stormed towards the penalty box. Even Julian couldn't keep up and so Kyle changed position. He was counting on a far shot, and I'm sure he would have held it. But the midfielder played towards the left where Fabio appeared out of nowhere, took a shot and scored.

It was suddenly quiet. One to nothing ... in the very first minute. The fast food drive-thru owner grinned smugly; Alex's and Kyle's fathers furrowed their brows; and Giacomo Ribaldo jogged past us, satisfaction plastered all over his face.

We were in shock. But then we remembered the dare on the old wooden bridge, and ran towards the center and prepared for our turn. Kevin made a speed pass to Tyler, who moved the ball forward. Danny was right there, caught the ball with his knee and stormed towards the *Furies'* goal. He didn't even have to check where Kevin stood. He could feel it, knew it in his bones from our practice, and indeed, the ball reached its destination. Kevin took control of it as he was still turning, convinced he'd have a clear shot at the goal. But instead, three *Furies* defenders were glued to his heels. The grass was no longer green. Wherever he looked, all he saw were red jerseys. Our enemies were all around him, making sure none of his team-mates were free. As Larry had predicted, it seemed as if 28 players were on the field. Before Kevin grasped what was happening, he lost the ball and the *Furies* counterattacked.

They skimmed the ball to Fabio a second time. This time he played to the right, and we expected him to pass to the front, close to the goal. But instead, the ball flew high above us to the other side, behind us. From there, the *Furies'* left forward headed the ball back to Fabio, who didn't hesitate. He volleyed the ball into the right corner.

Two nothing, less than three minutes into the game. We looked at each other. This was worse than the game against Mickey and his *Unbeatables*, and in that game we had been paralyzed by fear. But this time fear wasn't to blame; we had conquered our fear the night before.

This time our impending doom had a different reason. The *Furies* were simply better than us. They were in a league of their own, and the heart and engine of their league was Fabio.

Secretly I scanned the field for him and was startled when I finally spotted him. Fabio was watching me, too. He was jogging slowly towards his half of the field, but he wouldn't take his eyes off me. His gaze wasn't laced with mockery or ridicule. All I saw was helplessness. Suddenly his left foot bent sharply, Fabio screamed in pain and went down for a moment, and then limped off the field without a word.

"This is our chance," we all thought immediately, and Kevin translated that chance into action. Instead of passing back to Tyler, he stormed forward, right into the center of the defense, attracted three *Furies*, suddenly darted sideways, and then passed to the right to Danny. Like a bullet, Danny stormed toward the *Furies'* goal and fired. As if on a string, the ball flew 60 feet straight towards the goal, hit the left goal post with a bang, and then bounced into the goal.

Two to one. We had broken the ice. Kyle held the next two shots on our goal the way Tim Howard does, and then I came onto the field. I played right, raced past two enemies and sent the ball straight to Kevin. He heeled the ball to Roger, who gracefully thanked him. With his left foot, just like he did against the *Unbeatables*, he pounded the ball into the net.

"Two to two! Sweet! We've got them," Danny cheered us on as we fell back towards our side of the field to brace against the counterattack. But in no time the *Furies* took the lead and held it until just before half time. That's when they fouled Kevin in the penalty box. Alex, the man with the hardest kick in the world, took the shot and gunned the ball above the wall into the left upper corner. But there was a good reason why the *Furies'* goalie stood in the *Furies'* goal box. He flew straight towards the ball and looked as if he was trying to catch it. That was his mistake. Alex's shots cannot be caught that easily. You had to pound them away. Kevin knew that, and so he just stood there, ready, like Conor Casey, waiting for the ricochet, straddling it right into the net.

Three to three! This was fun. At least we thought so, and so did our parents. Even Kyle's father seemed to be caught up in soccer fever. We could see our sponsors, led by Alex's father, approach Larry to negotiate. But two of our spectators were anything but happy. The fat fast-food drive-thru owner was gulping down his third burger trying to drown his sorrow, and Giacomo Ribaldo's face had darkened with every goal. When the half time whistle blew, he couldn't stay away any longer. He interrupted his warm-up and marched over to his son.

Fabio's True Colors

During half time we sat around Larry sipping our
lemonades. There wasn't much to talk about. Everything
had worked in our favor. Since there were no mistakes
on our part, we had time to follow the conversation
between Fabio and his father.

They were too far away for us to hear a word, but it
was plain to see they were fighting.

"What's *his* problem?" Danny asked. "Fabio is injured."

"He's afraid he's going to lose," Kevin grinned.

But Larry pushed his cap far back and scratched his
forehead.

"I don't know. I don't think so. Just now, when Kevin
scored the three to three, Fabio was dancing for joy, and
I don't think you can dance like that with an injured
foot. What do you think?"

"I think we need to win!" Kevin said and everyone
agreed. After all, our jerseys and our future were on
the line. If we lost today, Alex's dad would confiscate
them and we'd be busy paying our debts for the next six

endless months. Then it would be winter and there'd be no soccer until spring. None of us wanted that. I didn't want that either, but something inside me resented what was happening.

"Kevin is right, " I said. "We should win, but not because someone is letting us win."

Then I stood up. I ignored my friends' objections and walked straight towards Fabio and his father. He was in the process of taking off his son's cleats to check the ankle, which, quite obviously, was not injured at all. "Okay, what's going on over here?" I asked without even saying hello first.

Fabio looked from me to his father and this time he didn't shrink.

"I want the *Wild Soccer Bunch* to win," he said furiously. "Then I'll get to play with you, and that's what I've wanted all along. But he wouldn't let me. He said I shouldn't have anything to do with you."

I looked at Fabio's father.

"Is that true?" I asked, but Giacomo Ribaldo, the Brazilian star striker, wouldn't lower himself to answer me. Instead he put his son's cleats back on.

"And now listen carefully, son. I expect you to give it your all and play as well as you can. Is that clear?"

Fabio looked at me for help.

"Is that *clear*?" his father repeated. But it was I who answered for my long lost friend.

"Crystal clear, sir." My eyes stayed focused on Fabio. "We don't need anybody's help. But I've never met a father who stands in the way of his son's happiness."

I looked Ribaldo straight in the eye.

"Fabio is my friend. And you can't do a thing about it. Is *that* clear?"

With one more shattering glare at Ribaldo, I walked back to my team. Kevin welcomed me back, spitting venom at me.

"What was *that* all about?" he hissed. "If Fabio plays, we'll lose."

"Maybe," I said. "But we just won something way more valuable. Kyle was right. It was Fabio's father. He was against us the whole time. Fabio is still our friend."

Kevin stared at me, his wrath still rising. But it was no longer directed at me; it was meant for Ribaldo, and when I looked at the ranks of the *Wild Soccer Bunch,* I noticed that everyone agreed with me. And then the referee called us to the field for the second half.

Dead End

It was our fury that fueled us. Even Fabio, who was playing again, couldn't stop Joey. He played like a magician, jumped over all feet that tried to stop him and sent a pass to Kevin. Kevin forced himself into the *Furies'* penalty box, and I worried that his ferocity would make him the stubborn ball hog we all knew, and he'd get caught in his enemy's feet. But not this time. He passed the ball to Tyler. Tyler appeared out of nowhere, as if he was wearing an invisibility cloak, expertly picked up the ball and directed it above the *Furies'* goalie right into the net.

Three to four. We were in the lead! I'm sure we would have celebrated even more and more loudly had we known that this was the last time in this game we'd be in the lead.

The *Furies* attacked. They were furious, too. They had not yet forgotten about the newspaper article, and they had Fabio back on the squad. Fabio had won ten new friends during half time, and he played like a

God. Although Julian was everywhere and every single one of us, even Kevin, fought past the point of sheer exhaustion, we slinked off the field after a bicycle kick, one header, two flying headers, one volley, and a devastating goal scored with the heel. The *Furies* won 11-4.

Ribaldo proudly carried his son on his shoulders, surrounded by his cheering team. We sneaked past the fast food drive-thru owner. The other sponsors had left long ago. Even Kyle's father fled in embarrassment. In the locker room we were finally alone.

We took a shower without saying a single word. The warm water felt good, but when we came back into the locker room, Alex's father was waiting for us, our jerseys already packed in his bag.

"I'm sorry," he said. "You fought hard; I have to hand it to you! But..." Then he sadly shook his head and left, taking with him the suitcase with our jerseys.

All's Well as Long as You're Wild

We licked our wounds that afternoon. Lying in the grass in front of Larry's stand, we wondered how we'd repay our debt. We had to do without soccer for six months now. That was cruel and unusual punishment, but we didn't regret a thing. It was our own decision and it was worth it. We won Fabio's friendship. We realized that he was lonely, and that his father was to blame. But things would change now, and we couldn't wait for Monday to roll around. We'd see him at school and we could play at break, even though his father didn't want him to.

But Fabio was not at school on Monday. He skipped school without an excuse, and the rumor was that he might not come back at all. Maybe his father had sent him to another school to make sure he wouldn't hook up with us.

Sad and disappointed, we trotted home that day. Danny had to help his mother clean the house. He'd get two dollars and fifty cents for that. Alex had to watch his sister for a dollar an hour. That meant playing mommy-daddy-Barbie for hours on end. Tyler and Kevin had to clean their room for the same amount of money. Roger helped his mother in her office, feeding old files to the shredder. He'd get 10 cents per pound. Julian and Josh had to paint the bathroom and kitchen to fix what they'd done during their spring cleaning efforts. They were paid nothing, of course. Joey had no way of making money either. His mother was too poor. And the only rich kid among us, Kyle, had disappeared. Exactly as he predicted, from now on he would be spending his time on the golf course.

But then everything changed. One afternoon all of us received a written invitation. All except Kyle's father, who received a call on his mobile phone, because he was on the driving range with his son.

An hour later all of us, Larry and our parents included, gathered outside the huge iron gate on a street called Heaven's Gate.

The gate with the big 9 opened elegantly, making way to a view of a garden party. The place was decorated impeccably; there were tables and chairs, all occupied by players of the U.S. national team: stars like Michael Bradley, Tim Howard, Clint Dempsey, and Landon Donovan who were in town for a training camp.

They were waiting for us, and as we approached they applauded. And then suddenly they all fell silent as Fabio and his father appeared on the balcony in front of them.

Giacomo Ribaldo cleared his throat and scratched his forehead, like Larry.

"I'm so glad you could come," he began, "I have to admit, I wasn't very friendly the last time you were here. I am truly sorry for that and I hope I can make it up to you with this party. You see, we have a great reason to celebrate. My son, who has been very lonely for a long time, has found ten good friends. What is special about these friends is that they all play for the best soccer team in the world."

We were flabbergasted.

He looked at us, from one to another, stopping on Kevin, who had fought so hard for us.

"You were right, Kevin. Even without Fabio and even without a victory against the *Furies*, you have shown us all what it takes to be a great team. I should have known better. I myself played on a team like yours at home, in Brazil. So I must ask your forgiveness, and I hope with all my heart that you will let Fabio play for the *Wild Soccer Bunch* again."

We cheered wildly and applauded until our hands hurt.

Then Fabio put a familiar suitcase on the terrace railing. He beamed with pride and joy. "Well guys, now we can play for real, because my father has just agreed to become our sponsor."

There was more cheering as he opened the suitcase and took out a jersey. It looked different. It had gotten a major facelift. Fabio turned it around, and there, in bright orange, emblazoned across the back, was a name and a number. It was incredible. We were speechless and only managed to murmur and whistle. And when Giacomo Ribaldo called each one of us up to get a jersey, everyone applauded.

Kevin would wear the 9. That's how Giacomo Ribaldo, one of the world's greatest soccer players—who wore the same number—showed his respect. Tyler would wear the 10, Kyle the 1, Julian the 8, Alex the 11, Danny the 4, because that was his favorite number, and Joey was happy with the 12. Fabio had chosen the 19, Roger would wear the 99 because he's so unpredictable, and Josh would wear the 00, being the wild card.

I was last, and before Giacomo Ribaldo gave me my jersey, he asked for attention.

"I've chosen the number 7 for Diego," he said. "It's a magical number. Perhaps it's because I'm from Brazil, but after what he's done for Fabio, for me, and for the *Wild Soccer Bunch*, I really do believe that Diego the tornado... has magical powers."

Applause erupted like a volcano and I blushed. But thankfully it didn't last very long. Dinner was ready and the waiters called all parents to the table—our parents, but not us, because we were busy playing soccer.

We played wearing our new jerseys, and this time Fabio played with us. And you won't believe this; we played against Michael Bradley, Tim Howard, Clint Dempsey, and Landon Donovan, the star players of the *U.S. World Cup Team*. Yes, that's who we played, and because there were lights everywhere, we played long into the night.

JOACHIM MASANNEK

Joachim was born in 1960 and studied German and Philosophy in college. He also studied at the University of Film and Television and worked as a camera operator, set designer and screenwriter in films and television.

His children's book series *The Wild Soccer Bunch* has been published in 28 countries. As the screenwriter and director of the five *The Wild Soccer Bunch* movies, Joachim has managed to bring about nine million viewers into the theatres. He was the coach of the real *Wild Bunch Soccer* team and the father of two of the players, Marlon (Tyler) and Leon (Kevin).

JAN BIRCK

Jan was born in 1963 and is an illustrator, animation artist, art director (advertising, animation, CD-ROM's), cartoonist, and CD-ROM designer. Jan designs the *Wild Soccer Bunch* merchandising with Joachim. Jan lives in Munich with his wife Mumi and his soccer playing sons Timo and Finn.

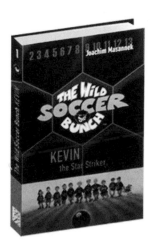

THE WILD SOCCER BUNCH
BOOK 1
KEVIN the Star Striker

When the last of the snow has finally melted, soccer season starts!

Kevin the Star Striker and the *Wild Soccer Bunch* rush to their field. They have found that Mickey the bulldozer and his gang, the *Unbeatables*, have taken over. Kevin and his friends challenge the *Unbeatables* to the biggest game of their lives.

Can the *Wild Soccer Bunch* defeat the *Unbeatables*, or will they lose their field of dreams forever? Can they do what no team has done before?

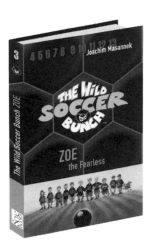

THE WILD SOCCER BUNCH
BOOK 3
ZOE the Fearless

Zoe is ten and soccer-crazy. She spends each day dreaming of becoming the first woman to play for the U.S. Men's National Soccer Team. Her dad believes in her dream, and encourages her to join the *Wild Soccer Bunch*. Even though Zoe would be the only girl on the team, she knows she could be their best player. But the *Wild Bunch* is not open-minded when it comes to welcoming new teammates, especially when they are girls...

Zoe's dad has a plan. He organizes a birthday tournament and invites the *Wild Bunch*. They present Zoe with a pair of red high heels, expecting her to make a fool of herself during the tournament. Zoe gladly accepts her gift. She wears the heels during the biggest game of her life, and proves that she's got what it takes to be a wild, winning member of the *Wild Soccer Bunch*.

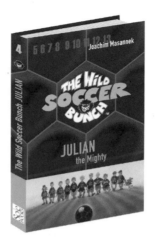

THE WILD SOCCER BUNCH
BOOK 4
JULIAN the Mighty

Julian Fort Knox, the All-In-One defender, is searching for his father who left one day and never returned. Along the way, Julian runs into Mickey the bulldozer and his gang and when they close in for the attack, the *Wild Soccer Bunch* is right there to help. One for all and all for one! The *Unbeatables* decide to challenge them to a rematch -- an all-or-nothing "Match for Camelot." Sure, the *Wild Soccer Bunch* beat them once, but can they do it again?

The Wild Soccer Bunch
JUNIOR CHAMPIONS CLUB

Join the coolest club in the world!

Thank you for being a fan of the Wild Soccer Bunch!

You are invited to join our Junior Champions Club at:

www.wildsoccerbunch.com/jc

As a member of the Junior Champions Club, you get:

* The newest books in the series before everyone else!
* Rewards and prizes!
* Wild Soccer Bunch news and updates!
* And much more!

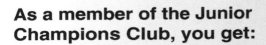

Visit our web site for The Wild Soccer Bunch experience

www.wildsoccerbunch.com

Love to read, live to play!

Selected Reviews for Books 1 and 2:

"The Wild Soccer Bunch, book 1, is a mash-up of 'The Mighty Ducks' and 'The Seven Samurai' that every soccer mom will want on her child's reading list!"
—STEVEN E. DE SOUZA, SCREENWRITER,
48 HOURS, DIE HARD

"A soccer-centric, middle-grade series that's been making waves abroad is arriving in the U.S. There are now more than nine million copies of the books in print in 32 countries."
—PUBLISHER'S WEEKLY

"This book is a clear winner."
—AMANDA RICHARDS, TOP AMAZON REVIEWER

"A Great Read for Middle School Students! I am a middle school librarian and the students absolutely love the first book in the series "Kevin the Star Striker." There is nothing else like this series that I can find that is readable and appealing to the low and average middle school reader."
—C. THOMKA, SCHOOL LIBRARIAN

"A fun and exciting read for young soccer fans, *The Wild Soccer Bunch* is a top pick."
—MIDWEST BOOK REVIEW

"This is the kind of book that gets kids reading and begging their parents for the next book in the 13-book series."
—ROBIN LANDRY

"This is one of those books where you'll have a hard time putting it down; you will want to read the entire book once you start."
—Shawn's Sharings

"As a retired teacher, who has taught many reluctant readers, I highly recommend this inspiring book."
—Educationtipster

"A shorter read, which means that even reluctant readers will not be intimidated. The story moves at a quick pace… Great humor… wonderful illustrations. My picky 9-year old said he would read more in the series (this is huge!!!)."
—An Educator's Life

"If your child goes to bed wearing soccer cleats so they won't miss one minute of field time in the morning, he or she will fall in love with the *Wild Soccer Bunch.*"
—JennyReviews.com

"This middle-grade novel isn't only fun and funny, it touches on some serious aspects of life."
—Imagination-Cafe Blog

"The writing is infectious and bodes well for a continuing series by this talented duo of Masannek and Brick."
—Grady Harp, Top Amazon reviewer

"*The Wild Soccer Bunch* is at it again and their humorously exciting antics will thrill the young reader."
—D. Fowler, Amazon top 50 reviewers, Vine Voice